Such Deliverance as This

Rebecca Velez

Such Deliverance as This

Published in the U.S. by Rebecca Velez Books
Manchester, NH

Cover image istockphoto.com/photo/arabic-woman-gm488598439

ISBN: 978-1-7322921-2-3

Library of Congress Control Number: 2018905563

For all my girlfriends who've encouraged me on life's journey, especially Linda, JoAnn, and our circle of moms in Billerica, MA. I hope I've blessed you too.

Cast of Characters

(Historical figures in bold)

Adin—Ezra's youngest daughter
Adlai—Ammonite goatherd
Ariel—Naama's husband
Artaxerxes—King of Persia 465-424 BC
Artystone—Naama's mother, a weaver of Persian rugs
Barak—Jarah's uncle
Benjamin—Jewish husband of Judith
Carmela—Gibeonite married to Benjamin's eldest brother
Ctesias—Persian merchant
Dael—Benjamin's third brother
David—the high priest's second son
Eden—Johanan's Jewish wife
Eli—the high priest's third son
Eliashib—high priest in the Jerusalem temple
Esther—Persian queen
Ezra—leader to Judah in 458 BC
Gili—Ariel's cousin
Hadassah—Ezra's eldest daughter
Hannah—Jarah's youngest cousin
Joiada—the high priest's eldest son
Jarah—Jew who returns to Judah
Jedidiah—Hadassah's deceased husband
Judith—Ammonite woman
Mary—Benjamin's youngest sister
Menachem—Tova's husband
Meremoth—priest in Jerusalem
Miriam—Ezra's third daughter

Naama—proselytized Jew who returns to Judah
Nehemiah—king Artaxerxes' cupbearer
Pazit—Jarah's maternal aunt, Barak's wife
Rachel—Ezra's deceased wife; mother of Hadassah, Rebekah, Miriam, and Adin
Rebekah—Ezra's second daughter
Tova—Ammonite woman married to a Jew
Tobiah—Ammonite, Judith's brother

Glossary

Ahura Mazda—Zoroastrian deity of good
Apadana—Persian king's audience chamber
Bet 'amma—house of the people, later called a synagogue
Cubic—an ancient measurement of about 18 inches
Daric—Persian coin
Em—Hebrew word for mother
Kohl—black eye make-up
Magus (pl. magi)—priest of Ahura-Mazda
Matok –Hebrew word for sweet one
Moloch—Ammonite god
Parasang—Persian measure of distance, about 3 miles
Qanat—irrigation pond
Softa—Hebrew word for grandmother
Yehud—the Persian satrapy (district) that included Judah

Jewish time

First watch   sunset to 9 p.m.
Second watch 9 p.m. to midnight
Third watch   midnight to 3 a.m.
Fourth watch   3 a.m. to sunrise

Such a Hope Series

Such a Time as This
Such Deliverance as This
Such Redemption as This

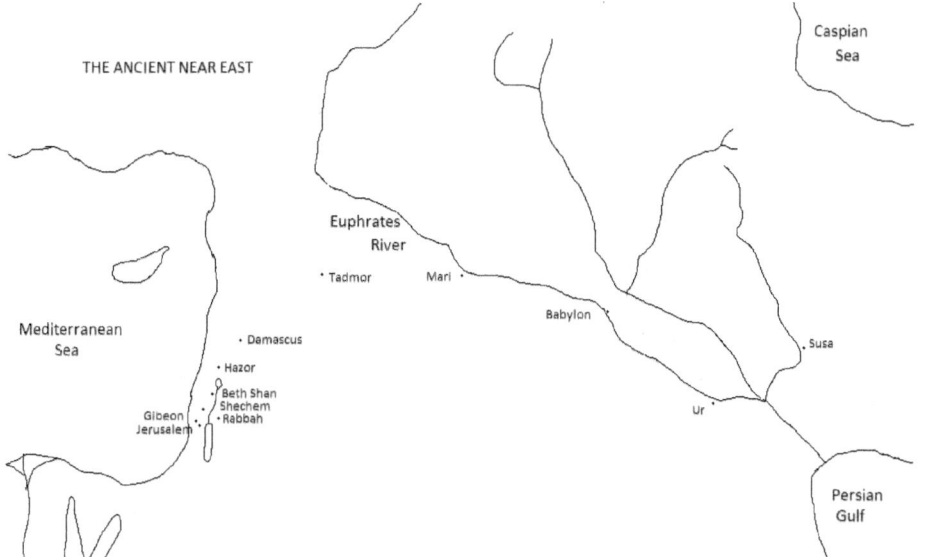

THE ANCIENT NEAR EAST

Caspian
Sea

Euphrates
River

· Tadmor   Mari ·

Mediterranean
Sea

Babylon ·

· Damascus

· Susa

· Hazor

Beth Shan
Shechem
· Rabbah

Gibeon
Jerusalem

Ur ·

Persian
Gulf

House of Ezra

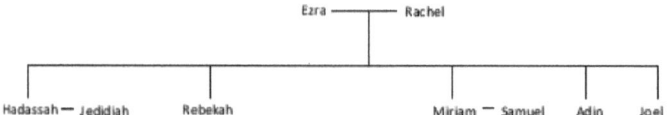

Ezra ——— Rachel

Hadassah — Jedidiah   Rebekah   Miriam — Samuel   Adin   Joel

Family of Naama

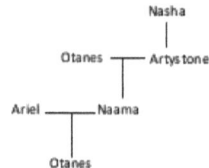

Nasha

Otanes ——— Artystone

Ariel ———— Naama

Otanes

House of the High Priest

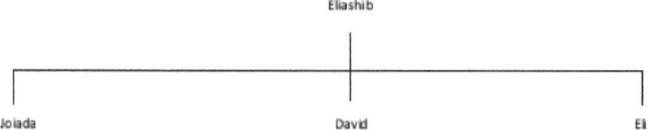

Eliashib

Joiada   David   Eli

Family of Oren

Jehu   Dan   Oren — Jarah   Elizabeth

Family of Benjamin

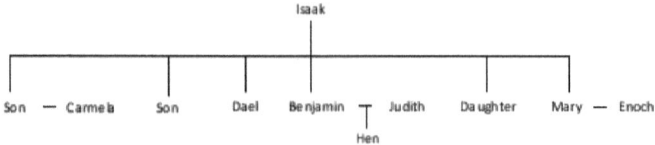

Isaak

Son — Carmela   Son   Dael   Benjamin — Judith   Daughter   Mary — Enoch

Hen

You our God have punished us less than our iniquities deserve, and have given us such deliverance as this. Ezra 9:13, NKJV

Chapter 1

J udith inhaled the heady scent of grapes. She hoped this crop, her first as a married woman, would produce an abundance of wine, a good omen for her marriage. She searched for her husband among the vines. Although tall for a woman, she couldn't see over them.

Would she be able to sneak up on him, or would he pounce on her first? It was dusk. His work was done for the day, and his nephews who helped in the vineyard had returned to their homes. A lentil stew bubbled on the hearth of their cottage, but it could wait until other appetites were satisfied.

As usual, Benjamin pinpointed her location and jumped out of the vines' shadows. She turned to greet him, but was caught short by the hard look on his face.

"Get behind me," he hissed.

Startled by his demeanor, Judith gave him as wide a berth as the rows of vines afforded, anticipation turning to fear. Scared she would be on the receiving end of some rough attention tonight, her mind scrambled for excuses. Could she plead that dinner would burn if they didn't return to their fire?

Benjamin grabbed her arm and shoved her behind his back, shielding her with his taller frame. Confused, she realized he was focusing on something beyond her, at the end of the row. When he bent to pick up fist-sized stones, she glimpsed glowing amber eyes and recoiled. A lioness!

"Turn around and walk slowly. Make sure there's nothing for me to trip over because I need to face her," Benjamin commanded softly.

Judith had never seen a lion from mere paces away, although

she had glimpsed them on the other side of her family's flock of goats. Her brothers had always managed to run them off before they mauled more than one or two kids. Swallowing noisily, she ripped her gaze from the cat's whiskered face and turned, looking for obstacles in the path. When she stooped to remove a stout branch, she whispered, "I found a sturdy-looking rod."

"Good. Hold onto it. I have these stones and my knife."

Judith breathed a little easier thinking of the half-cubit knife Benjamin sharpened every night after their evening meal. She felt better with the stick in her hand too. Halfway down the row, Benjamin launched a rock at the child-sized cat. Judith heard the stone hit earth and sensed her husband stoop to grab another.

"She's still coming. That didn't scare her off," Benjamin muttered.

"We're almost to the main path," Judith said.

"When we get there, we'll keep moving slowly, back-to-back. Don't forget to clear my path."

The couple shuffled awkwardly to their door, stumbling only once. The feline chose to remain between the rows of vines rather than pursue them on the open path. As soon as they both entered their home, Benjamin slammed the stout wooden door shut and wiped the sweat from his forehead. He grabbed Judith and kissed her.

"Well," she said.

"Never seen a lion before?"

"Not that close."

"They come into the vineyard from time to time. There's nothing but wilderness beyond us."

Judith pictured the scrubby trees and rocky hills beyond their vines and shuddered. Living at the edge of Gibeon afforded privacy and exposure.

"You should carry this walking stick whenever you're in the vineyard." Benjamin retrieved the carved oak from a corner of their front room. "Smells good," he said appreciatively, inhaling the aroma of the bubbling stew.

Judith stared open-mouthed from him to the stick he was offering.

"Are you all right?" he asked.

"I don't care to picture lions stalking me in the vineyard."

"She'll probably wander off tonight. Cats have a large range. Let's take a lighted torch and bring the goats in for the night. If she doesn't find food, she's likely to move on. You take this." He lit a pitchy branch and passed it to her. "And bring the walking stick and some rope. I'll hitch up my robe to carry rocks. We'll tie the rope around the goats' necks so we can bring them back in one group."

When they reached the goat pen, Benjamin handed Judith the rope and took the torch. "I'll keep watch while you tie this around their necks."

Judith fumbled with the twisted flax. *Take a deep breath. Calm now.* She managed to slip make-shift harnesses over the goats' heads and tighten the knots.

"Come along," she told the four goats. "You're not safe out here."

"Can you manage the goats?" Benjamin asked.

"I think so." *Please, Moloch, let them behave and get us safely inside.*

As they enjoyed their stew, barricaded within the thick limestone walls of their home, Judith admired her husband in the firelight, noting his muscled arms. She would not feel this safe tomorrow outside their home unless she stayed close to Benjamin. But tonight she felt protected and cherished.

Benjamin guarded Judith for a week, but they saw no more signs of the predator. He even walked to town with her to haul water. They were able to carry twice as many clay pots and needed to go only in the morning instead of Judith's accustomed runs morning and evening. The women ribbed him about doing a woman's work, especially his sister Mary, but when he told them about the lion, exaggerating its size, they shivered and cast jealous eyes on Judith.

Would their husbands protect them this well? Judith thought smugly. *And Benjamin was by far the most handsome man in the village.*

∞∞∞∞

Several moons later, after the vines were stripped of their fruit and the leaves had started to curl and fall, Judith was returning from town with water for washing clothes and blankets. When a twig snapped behind her, she turned, expecting to see Benjamin creeping up on her. Instead she faced a male lion three times the size of the last beast. It crouched, ready to spring.

Screaming, she threw the heavy water pot at its whiskered nose and ran for the house. She feared she would never reach the end of the row, but just as she reached its relative safety, her sandal snagged, and Judith fell forward. She could hear the lion's heavy breathing and curled into a protective ball. *Have mercy, Moloch, Adonai, whoever's the god of the lion.*

The shriek pierced Benjamin's heart. He grabbed his pruning hook more tightly and ran to the end of the row, struggling to pinpoint the location of his wife's cry. A feline yowl of pain split the air, giving him direction. As he sprinted up the central path, his wife fell into the dust at the other end of the vineyard. Adrenaline pushed him faster when he recognized the shape emerging from the row beside her. The caramel-colored beast's ribs showed through its coat, but it paused to sniff her sandals.

Benjamin bounded forward, intent on its eyes. If he didn't aim true, Judith would be mauled. A cubit's length from her head, he thrust the sharp iron blade on the tip of the hook at the lion's left eye. It caught at the inner eye and raked above the nose and into the right eye. Blinded, the cat screamed and lunged. Benjamin grabbed his knife from his belt and thrust upward with all the strength of his left arm, lodging it in the beast's chest.

The lion crumpled on the heaped form of his wife. Blood

flowed over her back as she struggled to get up.

"Stay still," Benjamin commanded, shoving the animal off her and standing over it with his hook. It twitched and then stilled. Benjamin pulled his knife from its body, eying his enemy.

Satisfied it was dead, he helped his sobbing wife to stand, snatching off her headdress and the outer robe covered with sticky blood. He examined the back of her head gently, her torso and down the backs of her legs to assure himself the lion's paws and teeth had not injured her. *None of the blood was hers, praise Adonai!* He grabbed her close, encircling her in his arms. When her legs buckled, he scooped her up and carried her home.

Crying, Judith nestled against her husband's chest. She hadn't been able to say anything coherent since the lion landed on her, and she couldn't stop shaking. Benjamin gently laid her on their sleeping pallet and wrapped her in their warmest woolen blanket. He heated water in a clay pot and made an aromatic tea from the small pots of herbs she kept on the mantle.

As she watched him struggle with the unfamiliar tasks, she stopped shivering and whispered, "You saved my life."

"I'm your husband. I'm sworn to protect you. Praise Adonai that I was out in the vineyard with a sharpened pruning hook." Benjamin brought her tea and kissed her forehead. "You are my life. What would I do without you?"

Chapter 2

N aama, Naama!" Ariel called from the street.

Naama continued weaving. Why was he calling her like she was a dog? Couldn't he come to the back of the courtyard where she and her mother spent their days weaving rugs?

"I'm here with the looms, Ariel!" she answered with exasperation, glancing at her mother, who seemed not to notice her son-in-law's rudeness.

As soon as Ariel could see her, he boomed, "We're going to Gibeon, Naama!"

Naama dropped her shuttle. *Ay, that will cost me some time.* "What do you mean--we're going to Gibeon? Where's Gibeon?"

"It's in *Yehud.* We have three days, four at the most, to be ready for a journey of five to seven moons. We'll leave Susa with Ezra the priest and travel to Babylon where a larger group will join with us. Come. We have much to do."

Naama was speechless, almost. *How could he?* "We have orders for two rugs. I'm in the middle of one now. I can't just pack up and leave." She glared at him. "How will *em* go, with the pain in her joints?" She turned to her mother for support, but Artystone had tactfully withdrawn into their small home.

"I bought this donkey for our goods, but she can ride it," Ariel answered hastily.

"The pain in her knees is so bad she can barely rise in the morning after the fire is lit. How can she get up and mount a donkey every day for months on end?"

"Then she can stay here," Ariel answered with finality as he turned to lead the donkey to the watering trough, leaving

Naama gaping at his back.

When Ariel left, Artystone returned to the courtyard with a cool skin of water.

"Em, I can't go all the way to Jerusalem and leave you here. Who will help you with the rugs? Ariel is crazed. He thinks I will pack in a few days and leave you and everything I know behind." Naama's voice held a hint of panic.

"You *must* go with him. He is your husband," Artystone said gently. "You are blessed to have him." Her face took on a faraway look, as if she were remembering Otanes, the husband whom King Xerxes executed before Naama's birth. Artystone returned her gaze to her only daughter. "And we both know I can't go with you. My bones would not survive the trip."

Naama clung to her mother and cried.

"Your brothers will care for me. Your nieces are old enough to learn our craft. I do need you to work on this rug, though. Otherwise, I'll be hopelessly behind." Artystone bent to her daughter's loom to untangle the shuttle and threads.

Her mother was trying to get her to settle down to the soothing rhythm of the loom. She felt mutinous, but even if her mother stayed up late for an entire moon she would never finish her own rug and Naama's on time. She must do this last task to help her mother. She would never see her again. Naama choked back a sob and took up the shuttle.

After working in silence until shadows filled the courtyard, Artystone said, "Let's prepare our meal. I have much to tell you. Who is leading this group back to Yehud?"

"I think Ariel said Ezra."

"He's a good man. He's the reason you are a Jew."

"What do you mean?"

"Our ancestors were not Jews."

Naama's thoughts whirled. The only grandparent she had known was her mother's mother, midwife to the king's harem. Nasha had not been Jewish. She had not observed Sabbath or attended the *bet 'amma*. Naama remembered visiting her grandfather's grave and leaving gifts of flowers. Nasha kept the trips

7

from her daughter by telling her granddaughter it was their secret, a special time they shared. Naama had not realized until she became an adult that they had been performing pagan Persian rites.

Artystone continued, "After your father was executed, I was lonely. I didn't find comfort in the Zoroastrian rites for the dead. And then I met the personal God of the Jews. He cared about *me*. He took care of *me*, a lowly widow. We couldn't pay our rent. He provided an entire year's rent. I still don't know how. He is an amazing God, daughter. He took me on a path I never imagined, and now he's taking you in a different direction—to the Promised Land. Every Jew dreams of going home, and you get to go. It's a blessing, daughter."

"Feels more like a curse," Naama mumbled.

"Blessings are often birthed through pain, just like babies."

Naama studied her stooped, gray-haired mother. She feared the pain would burst her heart.

∞∞∞

"She doesn't want to go!" Ariel explained in disbelief to his cousin Gili.

"Did you tell her we have land there? Vineyards?"

"No, she didn't want to hear it. And I doubt she'd care. She's a skilled rug maker. She doesn't want to become a laborer in a vineyard, which is what we'll all be for the first years."

"But our grandfather chose the two of us to return to reclaim our family's inheritance! It's an honor."

"I know it's an honor, Gili. But right now it's an honor that's making my head ache!"

Chapter 3

King Artaxerxes entered his private dining room. "Another son, Mother! Four fine sons! The gods must be smiling on me."

Esther decided to ignore her adopted son's reference to "the gods." She had an important request for Hadassah, so she simply remarked, "I held him today, and he seems healthy. At least he has a vigorous cry."

As the only banqueters, the two reclined on gold couches in the enormous candlelit room near doors opening to the palace gardens. Tonight they were closed against the chill, but the diners could admire the moon's shimmering reflection in the *qanat*. Two ebony African servants stood stiffly behind them to whisk away gold dishes after each course. The king's cupbearer Nehemiah sipped each goblet of wine before presenting it, and a pair of armed guards at the door monitored an old servant-woman who tasted food from each dish.

The tantalizing aroma of spicy meat tempted them to eat before further conversation. The camel meat reminded Esther of the banquet she prepared sixteen years ago for Artaxerxes' father King Xerxes. Her request on that night determined the fate of the Jews in the Persian Empire. She relaxed, remembering how Adonai had turned the king's heart "like channels of water." *He will help me now. He cares about Hadassah and her future even more than I do.*

Finally sated, the king said, "Ezra is assembling a small band that will leave Susa this week. Word's out for any Jew in this part of the empire who wishes to return to the land of his fathers to meet him at the irrigation canal Ahava in Babylon at the beginning of Nisan. He should be able to reach Babylon from here in about a moon's time."

Thank you, Adonai. Artaxerxes brought up the very subject I want to discuss. "My people will revitalize Yehud by increasing trade and revenue."

"They are excellent tradesmen. Allowing them to return is good policy."

"There's a palace servant I wish you'd consider releasing to return with Ezra."

"Which one?" Artaxerxes inquired languidly, choosing another plump date.

"Hadassah."

Her son's eyes snapped back to his mother's attractive face. Her green eyes were luminous, lit with sincere concern.

"Have you noticed how thin she's become since Jedidiah's death? I'm afraid she's going to fade away."

Artaxerxes tried to remember the last time he had seen the girl, a few years his senior. He had always been attracted to her and planned to add her to his harem after a year's period of mourning. When had her husband died? It had been during the winter, so it would be months before he could act on his plan. "I'll think on it, Mother."

Esther was relieved he had not denied her request outright. She had seen the way he looked at Hadassah, which was one reason she wanted the girl to return to Jerusalem with her father.

∞∞∞∞

The next day Artaxerxes sat on his balcony when the servant girls customarily strolled in the gardens. He easily spotted Hadassah, who had been his childhood playmate in his adopted mother's quarters. Hadassah was Esther's namesake, the daughter of her best friend Rachel and the priest Ezra. Officially, Hadassah was being trained for service, but in reality his mother reared Hadassah while Rachel endured one pregnancy after another until the last one weakened and eventually killed her. While his adoptive mother grieved over her barrenness, Hadassah had become the daughter of her heart.

Where Hadassah had gotten her beauty Artaxerxes couldn't fathom—none of her sisters came close. His mother was right, though. She had lost her curves and was pitifully thin. And she moved listlessly through the lush palace gardens, not picking the citrus or burying her face in the roses like her companions. *Should I let her go or make her part of the harem? There's not long to decide. Her father will be leading out his band in a few days.*

∞∞∞∞

Ctesias retired to the storage room in the back of his shop to speak with the king's steward, who claimed to carry vital news. The man provided him with regular information in exchange for employment for his daughters. *How many daughters does he have? When I hired the sixth girl last week, I beseeched the gods she wouldn't be as clumsy as her older sister who dropped nearly as many pieces as she sold.*

He regarded the black-glazed Athenian cups, bowls, and platters with satisfaction. No other importer in the palace city of Susa could lay hands on them. He controlled the market. Inhaling the pungence of the cinnamon and other spices stored on the shelves, he settled himself on a stool.

The steward began eagerly, "I heard the king say yesterday that Ezra's band leaves in three days."

Ctesias rubbed his beard thoughtfully. *This piece of information is worth the wages of every one of those girls. I'll corroborate it with other reports, but it's the first definite departure date I've heard.* If they were leaving in two days, he had a lot to wrap up before he could follow, dogging their footsteps, waiting for his opportunity.

"Why did it take so long to deliver this information?" he demanded with a vicious kick aimed at the servant's shins.

The fellow quickly sidestepped and bowed. "His Most Magnificent required my presence in the palace. This was the first I could slip away, and I must return before I am missed." He was gone before Ctesias could frame another inquiry or aim another blow.

Ctesias bellowed for his slave. "Go to Zanes' forge and collect the weapons he has for me. I need all of them tonight. Wrap the largest Athenian platter and four sets of tableware as payment. That should please him since it's more than we agreed on. Take a camel with you to haul the swords home, and hide the weapons in the stable. I'll leave in two days, three at the most."

Chapter 4

Judith hurried through her morning tasks, waved good-bye to her husband laboring in the vineyard, and set off for her friend's small limestone house in town. From the end of the dusty street she could see Tova scouring a pot, her face lined with frown lines. *She must have burnt Menachem's dinner again and soaked the pot overnight to loosen the mess. Poor Menachem! His wife presents him with a steady stream of burnt offerings.* Judith smiled at her wit. *But I never hear him complain. So different from how we grew up.* She shuddered, remembering her father's wrath when her mother had burned their food.

Shrugging off the memory, she called out a greeting to her friend. "*Shalom!* How are you feeling today?"

Tova patted her mounded belly. "Tired. This little one loves to kick at night when I'm trying to rest. How are you?"

"Happy! I'm going to visit my family." Judith's perfect oval face lit with pleasure. "Won't you come with me, Tova?"

Tova shook her head emphatically. "No! Who would care for my Menachem? Who's taking care of Benjamin? Besides, I need plenty of time to prepare for Passover."

"Benjamin's mother will feed him while I'm gone, and since we always eat Passover with them, I don't have much to do. I'll be back before Passover. Come, Tova. Your sisters miss you, I'm sure. And this will be the last time I can go home for a while. I have news." Judith grinned.

Tova stopped scraping the pot and looked expectantly at her childhood friend. They were both Ammonite, but their great-grandparents had pastured their flocks close to the Jordan River in order to take advantage of land left virtually empty by the

Israelites.

"I'm expecting a little one too!" Judith beamed.

Tova rose to hug her friend, nearly knocking the pot over with her ungainly movements. They laughed. "I'm not even big yet, and already I'm this clumsy. When do you think your baby will be born?"

"In the rainy season, maybe in Chislev. I've only missed one bleeding, but I feel sick every morning when I wake up, so I know."

"Of course you do. This is wonderful, Judith! Just think. Our children will grow up together. But why would you want to travel now, if you're already feeling sick? And how will you get back to your family?"

"A few Ammonite traders are leaving Gibeon tomorrow to return to Rabbah."

"But how will you find your family? They could be pasturing the goats anywhere."

"It won't be hard. They'll be close to the city for the new year's festival."

Realization and then horror registered on Tova's face as she gaped at her friend. "You're going for the rites to Moloch, aren't you?"

Judith tossed her headdress behind her shoulder. "I enjoy the festival. The region will be assured of a good harvest after the temple girl has conceived. And I plan to ask for a strong son. What's wrong with that?"

"There's nothing wrong with asking for a healthy child. I implore Adonai for this babe every day," Tova said, "But Moloch can't help you. He's a god of death."

"A good daughter of Ammon you've turned out to be." Judith whirled away.

Tova sat back on her heels as her friend stormed up the street. "I'm a daughter of Israel now," Tova whispered, "as I hoped you would become."

By the time Judith returned she would be full of news from

home and would have forgotten their tiff. Judith was like that—quick to argue but promptly forget the matter. *But I'll remember. I hoped Judith had left behind her old beliefs like I did.*

Tova resumed scrubbing the pot and cleaning the limestone plates her family had sent her when she married Menachem two harvests ago. That year had been her last at the so-called "holy marriage," which was anything but holy in her opinion. One of the city's elders had been chosen to lie with a temple prostitute to impregnate her and ensure the land's fertility for the coming year. Before she left for Gibeon as Judith's companion, everyone rejoiced over the prostitute's pregnancy.

In Gibeon, she heard about Adonai, His perfection and just laws. She was relieved when a devout Jew named Menachem offered a good bride price for her, and her family accepted. She would never have to return to Moloch's temple or altars again. Some of the Ammonite women still carried small cypress or oak idols, but no one worshipped him openly in Yehud.

Chapter 5

Esther leaned on Hadassah's arm as they strolled through fragrant roses in the palace gardens. Night was falling, and its coolness kissed their skin. "Hadassah, child, I have good news for you," Esther said, as they settled on a stone bench to stargaze. "Your family will not be leaving you behind after all."

Hadassah's dark pain-filled eyes searched her benefactress's face with a trace of hope. "Is one of my sisters marrying and staying in Persia?"

"No, better. You can go with them."

Hadassah appeared stunned. Esther saw hope flicker in her eyes. She had done well to secure her namesake's release from the palace.

"But I can't leave you, my queen. Who will apply your face paint and help you dress? Whose arm will you lean on as you walk in the gardens?"

Esther would miss Hadassah like one of her own arms. Hadassah might even pretend to leave and hide for a few weeks while the caravan left without her. She would emerge after enough time had elapsed so Esther could not send her to catch up with her father. Very well, she would give the girl a bit of a scare.

"Hadassah, if you stay here, Artaxerxes will make you part of his harem."

Hadassah looked at her in shock. "But . . . but . . . Jedidiah's only been gone three moons!"

"He'd wait awhile. But I've seen the way he looks at you. It would happen, and I don't think the harem's the best place for you."

"No, no! I thought I'd serve you for the rest of my life." Hadassah hid her face in her hands and drew deep, shuddering breaths.

"I'm quite a bit older than you, my dear. What would you do after my death?"

Hadassah's head popped up. "May Adonai grant you many more years."

"But someday I will leave you."

"I hadn't planned that far ahead," Hadassah admitted softly. "But I don't want to remarry!" she added forcefully.

"I know you don't, and I think that's why you should leave with your father. You know how absent-minded he is. Your un-married sisters care for him now, preparing meals and washing his clothes. Once those two marry, who will watch over your father? He feels like you do about remarriage."

Being forced into the harem would probably kill Hadassah, especially if she became pregnant in her weakened state. The best way to manage Hadassah was to appeal to her desire to serve someone else. *Could Hadassah survive the arduous trip and bloom again back in Jerusalem?* Esther considered the roses around them. The gardeners pruned them back to small bushes each year, but they flourished after each cutting. Surely women could do the same.

"Let's return to my rooms. I want to send gifts to the temple. I have linen cloth and some gold. I want you to have a length of cloth too. Someday you'll need a new tunic and robe. Your dresses may wear out on the journey." Esther glanced down at Hadassah's delicate footwear. "Do you own a sturdy pair of san-dals?"

"No."

"Send Mitra to the leather worker for two pairs. You've served me well."

"You're too generous, my queen."

"Nonsense, you are Rachel's daughter. She and your father have lent me your companionship for many years. I treasure their gift, and I will miss you." Esther paused, "But you *must* go."

Chapter 6

Benjamin missed his wife's warmth as soon as she rose before the dawn. Swinging his legs over the side of the sleeping platform, he studied his willowy, dark-haired wife as she gathered food for her journey. *I still can't believe my good fortune in marrying her. She's beautiful and an excellent cook. Best of all, she pleases me every night.*

Benjamin was the fourth son of a small landowner. His family held some influence in their town of Gibeon, but all the family land had been divided between the eldest two sons. The land barely supported their two families. And his eldest brother had three daughters he must provide dowries for! Dael, his third brother, had set out for Ammonite territory to try his hand at trade years ago.

"If I can acquire merchandise and send it for you to sell, the family fortune will increase," Dael said to convince his parents. Instead, he found a comfortable life with a merchant family who gave him one of their seven daughters in exchange for his labor. Apparently they were long on daughters and short on sons to maintain the family business. Dael adopted their family name as part of the marriage agreement, but even though there were three other sons to carry on his father's line, Dael's choices hurt his parents. Although his arrangement didn't benefit the family with goods to sell, it had benefitted Benjamin.

As a merchant, Dael made many contacts and kept an eye open for an advantageous situation for his younger brother. Benjamin visited Rabbah one year, and Dael presented various options, but Benjamin made it clear he wished to remain in the land of Yehud. Dael eventually heard of an Ammonite clan of goat herders who owned property in Gibeon but chose not to reside there.

He sought out Judith's family and extolled his brother's diligence, brawn and charm. He also arranged a meeting between Benjamin and his father and Judith's father and brothers. Its success resulted in a winter wedding and Benjamin's ownership of a vineyard complete with house. He couldn't express his gratitude to his brother adequately, though he tried with the best jar of wine he could afford. An amazing wife, a livelihood and house —all in his hometown!

His family, in turn, gave a bride gift of a dozen goats. Truth be told, they didn't know what to do with all those goats, but the ewes kept producing twins. Since Judith's family depended on their herds, both families prospered with the exchange.

Judith seemed to like him and the two-room house and vineyard, but she missed her past life. That was the reason Tova came during harvest time. Both of their families had lived nomadic lives herding animals, but they wintered in the same pastureland, and the two had been fast friends for as long as they could remember. So Tova had been sent to help at harvest and to ease Judith's homesickness. It was a short-term plan, but his boyhood friend Menachem had decided he liked the girl and offered the bride price for her. They married soon after the harvest was gathered, and Judith seemed more content with her friend's presence.

When Judith finished her preparations, Benjamin sadly kissed his wife. She smiled at him. "There's roasted grain this morning and leftover bread and goat cheese for when the sun is high. Tonight your family's expecting you, as they are every night until I return. I'll be home before you can finish clearing thistles from the new section of vineyard you're working on."

"So if I can finish in three days' time, you'll be back?" Benjamin asked hopefully, twirling her hair around his fingers.

"Now, Ben, you know I won't even have reached my family by then. And you'd have to work non-stop to accomplish that." She gave him another kiss.

"I'm going to miss you."

"I'll miss you too. I won't be making this trip again anytime soon, but I do need to go."

∞∞∞∞

Judith fingered the small oak idol hidden in the folds of her dusty robes. The sun had not started to set, yet they were almost to Jericho. They would spend a night here and continue across the Jordan to Rabbah, camping one more night before they reached their destination. Two other Ammonite women had joined the group setting off at daybreak. Judith was glad to see them since she had assured Benjamin there would be other women visiting their families at this time of year. A few women always returned for the festival.

Judith had not returned since her marriage three rainy seasons ago, but now she had an important request she wanted to present at the high place outside of Rabbah. After all, she had lost one child before it made its presence known by giving her a belly. She was glad she hadn't told Benjamin about that babe. She had kept this one a secret too, or he might not have allowed her to travel this far. She wanted to spare him disappointment if there were another loss, but she believed that if she could bring an offering to Moloch, he would grant her a healthy son. Her mother or one of her brothers would help obtain a fitting sacrifice.

On the third day, Judith found her family in tents pitched to the west of Rabbah. They welcomed her warmly, slaughtering and feasting on a goat to celebrate her safe return. Judith broached her need the next day as she sat with her mother, grinding barley into flour with mortar and pestle. "I need to bring a worthy sacrifice to Moloch. I couldn't ask Benjamin. He wouldn't understand."

Her mother pounded harder on the grain. Finally she wiped

sweat from her brow. "I wish I could help you, but your father favors his youngest wife. I can ask for nothing, Judith." Her mother's chin sank to her chest, and her veil hid her face.

For the first time, Judith noticed her mother's drab, worn tunic. She thought back to the previous night. Her mother had been sitting at the outskirts of the fire. As the guest of honor, Judith had received the best portion of meat, even before the men took theirs. She joined her mother, and her brothers came to talk with her, but her father and his other two wives stayed close to the fire. With shock, Judith wondered if her mother had eaten any of the meat she had spent hours preparing. All she remembered seeing her eat was bread dipped in oil.

Judith was still trying to digest these disturbing observations when her mother continued, "Maybe your brother Tobiah would help you. He's always been partial to you."

Trying to relieve her mother's distress, Judith answered quickly, "That's a good idea. I'll ask him. I'm sure he'll help."

When Judith walked to Tobiah's tent to talk with him, she noticed his prosperity. He had taken another wife since her absence. His first wife had produced two sons and a daughter, and it looked like a slave girl was doing the washing. *His flocks must be flourishing if he can afford a second wife and a slave.* Judith followed a goat path in the direction the girl had pointed. *I hope he's close. This goat dung and my stomach…bah!*

Moloch seemed to be smiling on her since her brother's flock appeared after a short walk. A slave guarded the far end of the animals' pasture to ward off predators and discourage strays. Tobiah was perched on a rock close to the path. He jumped down when he saw her.

"I brought you fresh bread and water from the spring," Judith offered.

"Just like old times. Thank you." Tobiah devoured the bread, washing it down with the pure water. "You've also brought something else, eh? News?" At Judith's startled look, he continued, "A niece or a nephew, I think."

How Tobiah always figured out such things, Judith couldn't

guess. He wiped his mouth on the back of his hand and continued. "If I'm not mistaken, you need a gift for Moloch."

At the sight of Judith's astonished face, Tobiah roared with laughter. "Both my wives are also with child." He sobered. "They each need a kid to sacrifice this year at the festival, so I can't help you."

Judith was disappointed but could appreciate her brother's situation.

"I do, however, have an idea." When Judith regarded him with interest, he asked, "Do you remember my friend Adlai?"

Judith nodded. Adlai was closer to her age than Tobiah's.

"He isn't married yet. He's built up a flock, though, and he's looking for a woman to warm his bed."

At first Judith missed what her brother was suggesting, but as realization dawned, she snapped, "I *am* married."

"Yes, and already pregnant, so no harm would be done. It would be a celebration of the festival. Look, I thought you wanted a good sacrifice. I'm just delivering a message. He was talking about you last night after he heard of your return." When Judith didn't respond, he said, "He's tending his flock over that hill. During the festival, he'll be in town. It's between you and him. I don't even need to know what you decide."

Judith spun on her heel and fled back the way she had come.

Chapter 7

Naama waited for her turn at the well, her heavy clay pot digging into her shoulder.

"Why don't you set that down while you're waiting, Naama?"

Naama turned woodenly toward the speaker. "Parmys!" She set the jar down and threw her arms around her childhood friend.

Parmys hugged her tightly. "You looked far away, and didn't even notice me."

"I'm going to be far away starting the day after tomorrow," Naama said bitterly.

"I wish it weren't so. Why do men have to yank us away from our peaceful lives? Don't they understand it tears us like we tear rags from cloth?"

"They must not have hearts. Ariel certainly doesn't."

Parmys studied her friend. "Do you have time to come say good-bye to the baby tonight?"

"I'll make time. I'm going to miss you so much, Parmys!"

As Naama headed to the street where Parmys lived, the stench of rotting refuse assaulted her. She was thankful for the protected courtyard with its fragrant citrus trees where she worked when it was warm. *What will our new home be like?* Since Ariel's land was a vineyard, she decided they would live outside the town. Maybe she could make rugs in the shade of the vines.

A group of women milled in front of the two-room mud-brick home where Parmys lived with her husband and baby. As she neared, she recognized several of her childhood friends. One called out, "Here she is." Another rushed to greet her with two lovely rose blooms and thrust the beauties into her hand.

"How thoughtful. And look! They're red, my favorite. Why are you all here?"

"To bid you a good journey, silly. Why else?" Parmys said, embracing her. "You might not see everyone at the well or in the market before you leave, so everyone came tonight."

Tears welled in Naama's eyes as she opened her arms for a group hug. "Where am I ever going to find such good friends?"

∞∞∞

One look at his wife's mutinous expression told Ariel he had better make room on the donkey for her precious rug. He wasn't sure how. He needed the tools for the vineyard, and there were three sleeping mats and blankets, crocks for cooking, barley, dried fruit, and other essentials. When he saw her eyes tear, he softened. "We'll figure it out."

"It's the smallest one in the house."

"I know. I'll get it to fit." They both looked helplessly at the already overloaded animal.

"Shalom," a voice cried. "Open the gate."

Relieved at the interruption, Ariel unlatched the gate to reveal Gili leading a donkey.

"Look, *matok*. The Almighty sent us exactly what we need. The donkey *is* for our trip, isn't he?" Ariel looked from his wife back to his cousin.

"Yes. Uncle Abiram gave her to us, and since this is a male, and you already have a female..."

"We'll have plenty of donkeys to work the land!" Ariel finished. The men slapped each other on the back.

"We can take turns riding too."

"Naama, bring the rug. It will fit over him as a blanket."

Naama wrinkled her nose.

"It will wash, won't it?"

Naama nodded and reached out to stroke the donkey between his ears. "What's his name, Gili?"

"I don't think he has one. Why don't you name him?"

Naama considered the gray and white animal. "Abi, I think, so we'll remember your uncle and how he helped us." She turned back to the house.

Ariel whispered, "That sure improved her mood. You showed up at the perfect time, Gili."

"You'd be wise to remember your wife likes gifts."

"I'll have the donkey to remind me. But let's not tell Uncle Abiram what its new name is."

"He might not take it well." The two men looked at each other and laughed.

"Why would she name a beast of burden after my uncle?" Ariel asked when he regained control.

"I don't know. Who can understand a woman?"

Chapter 8

"What do you mean the Bactrians are away?" Ctesias roared.

"A messenger arrived yesterday. They're in the desert at the funeral of their chieftain," answered Zanes.

"Did the messenger say where in the desert?"

"No. He said they would return in seven days."

"A week! Those cursed Jews started out yesterday. Killing them before they reach Babylon is the plan. We'll be hard pressed to catch up to them. I've been waiting for this opportunity for years, and now those unreliable nomads are going to spoil our plans."

Ctesias began pacing, his hands pressed to his head, spewing curses. This was the chance he had been waiting for to avenge his father's death. Oibares, along with Zanes' father Artasyras, had been killed in the Purim war fifteen years earlier when they supported the attack on the Jews. The Jews had soundly defeated their opponents, killing eight hundred men in Susa alone. "Isn't there someone else we could hire?"

"We wanted to hire men from out of the area, so no word of this would leak out. If the king gets wind of it, we're all dead," Zanes answered. "We can't put together another team of mercenaries spur-of-the-moment. I want my revenge as much as you. My family was disgraced, and like yours, went into debt, nearly losing the family business. We're barely respectable again. You know we can't do anything that will raise suspicion, Ctesias."

Ctesias grunted and kicked an earthenware pot, shattering it against the stone wall. "It's more than disgrace, Zanes. They killed my father!"

Zanes shushed him. "Not so loud. You'll give the whole business away. How long do you figure it will take them to reach Babylon?"

"It's only a few hundred people. They should reach Ur in about ten days and Babylon two weeks after that."

"Couldn't you still catch up with them if you're all mounted?"

"Possibly, but it's more populated the closer you get to Babylon. We wanted to take care of them in a desolate spot before they reached the river." Ctesias sighed.

"There are plenty of deserted places between here and Jerusalem."

"More men will join the group in Babylon. There's no way we could annihilate all of them. Have you been able to find out if they'll have weapons?" Ctesias asked the metalworker.

"My counterpart in Babylon says he filled an order for three hundred swords, and as many daggers. Sounds like each man will be armed."

"But they're traveling with women and children, which will make them more vulnerable."

"The real question is whether King Artaxerxes will send soldiers with them."

"Why would he do that?" Ctesias questioned sharply.

"Because of the treasure."

"What treasure?"

"The king's sending gifts to the Jews' god. There's a temple in Jerusalem."

"I've never seen a Jewish temple. They usually meet in a large home or business."

"Those are the *bet 'ammas*. There's only one temple."

"Strange people. Wouldn't it please their god to build him many places of worship?"

"You'd think so, but imagine how rich this temple must be since it's the only one."

Ctesias rubbed his beard thoughtfully. "Have you heard what

the king's offering the Jews' god?"

"Gold and silver."

Ctesias smiled greedily. "Better than sacrificial animals."

"For us, at least."

"I don't think our families will ever fall into debt again, my friend."

"The Bactrians will be pleased too. If they do their job well, they can take some of the spoils."

∞∞∞

Hadassah gazed at the brick ziggurat looming behind Ur's walls as she walked with her three sisters. Although tired from the day's travel, she felt content to be with her sisters, grateful she hadn't been separated from them forever.

"Father says this temple is for the moon god Nanna," Adin said.

"Their moon god didn't do them any favors from the look of things," Miriam declared, looking at the deserted landscape and derelict temple.

"The city used to sit at the mouth of the sea and the Euphrates, but now the water's receded," Hadassah explained.

"We should reach the Euphrates tomorrow," Rebekah said. "I can't wait to wash off this grime!"

"A little more dirt wouldn't hurt," Miriam cried. "Let's see who can get the farthest up the ziggurat!"

"Miriam, you can't do that!" Hadassah scolded.

"Why not? The moon god can't do anything about it!"

"But what about his worshippers?"

"There's no one in sight except us sons and daughters of Abraham. Plus if I climb up I can see what's ahead—the Euphrates and whatever else lies there."

"It looks steep. You might fall."

"I'll tag along and watch from the bottom," Adin said. "And we'll gather dried dung on the way back for the fire."

29

"Are you coming, Rebekah?" Miriam asked.

"No, but you go ahead. You'll be married and settled down before you know it," Rebekah said wistfully. Miriam set off at a run, Adin trotting behind her. "They'll be fine, Hadassah. Stop worrying."

"It's going to be hard when she marries and moves to Gibeon with her husband's family."

"We won't have to worry about her so much," Rebekah said with a slight smile.

"But I'll always be concerned about her. She's my little sister, as are you. At least you're staying in Jerusalem. We can still see each other, and you can eat some of your Sabbath meals with us, even if you spend time with your husband's family, too."

"Of course we'll come eat with you and *abba* and Adin. We'll make our favorite foods."

"Sabbath is always the best day of the week. I was always happy the queen let me come home on the Sabbath."

"And she sent fruit, flowers, or bread, so we were always glad to see you," Rebekah teased.

"Even if your tiny sleeping space was overcrowded!"

"Absolutely," Rebekah agreed, linking her arm through her sister's. "Someday I hope to crowd a room in my new home with as many children as I have sisters."

Chapter 9

W e need more wood," Joiada declared, surveying the small stack left in the Jerusalem temple's wood chamber.

"We need more help," his brother Eli said dismally. "There's too much work. My wife complains she never sees me. We labor until well past sundown every day, offering sacrifices for people. Sometimes we even get stuck carrying the water... or wood."

"We're the sons of the high priest," David said. "We do what needs to be done. I'll take a couple donkeys and look for wood this afternoon."

"I wish I could send someone with you, but Meremoth's sick, so the rest of us are already covering his duties," Joiada answered.

"It's all right. I like working outdoors."

"What we need is more Levites," Eli said. "Add that to your prayers this morning, Joiada."

"Could you request a few more priests too? The elders should be sitting in the courtyard dispensing wisdom, not lifting goats and bulls," David pointed out.

"I know, but we simply can't manage without them," Joiada said in frustration. "We've asked the exiles in Persia and Babylon to return to Jerusalem, but no groups have come since Zerubbabel returned sixty years ago."

"There's been some talk of a group coming soon," David said.

"That's been going on for years. Nothing ever seems to come of the talk." Joiada sighed.

"It would be a long trip through dangerous territory," Eli

mused.

Hadassah limped along, lost in memories of a happier time when Miriam ran up to her. "Look behind us, Hadassah!"

Hadassah turned. The company had been walking within view of the mighty Euphrates for over a week now, and the flat land allowed the travelers to see great distances. But now their view was obscured by an ugly dark curtain that cut them off from the world behind them.

"Isn't it the fiercest storm you've ever seen?" Miriam asked.

"I've never seen a sandstorm like it," Hadassah agreed. "Do you think it will catch us?"

"I'm going to ask abba."

Ctesias pressed his face into Jasper's flank, hoping the beast would not bolt. His stallion was fleet, but tended toward skittishness. It was getting hard to breathe. Above the wind's whistling, he heard faint pounding, probably a horse escaping. He gripped Jasper more tightly.

At least the camels carrying their supplies would simply kneel, close their eyes and nostrils, and patiently wait out the storm. He heard more hoof beats. How long would this storm and its aftermath delay them? They had been only half a day behind Ezra. Maybe this storm would do his work for him and destroy the Jews.

Finally, hours later, it abated. Ctesias coughed weakly and drank all the water in his goatskin in an effort to clear his throat of the grit. Feeling recovered enough to take stock, Ctesias began to move among the fifty men. One Bactrian had been trampled to death when the horses panicked and ran. Several others had been dragged as they struggled to control their crazed mounts. They were having trouble breathing due to the amount of sand they had inhaled. Ten mares were missing. Since the camels travelled more slowly and only caught up to the band at night, he didn't know how they and their drivers had fared, but he figured all was well since they excelled at desert travel.

They needed to locate the horses. And the Bactrians would want to honor their dead comrade. How long would those rites take?

Zanes caught up to him. "The horses should be easy to find. They probably headed toward water. I'll send a few men down to the river, and others toward the setting sun to look for any springs that way."

"Good. We'll set up camp by the river and wait for the camels. The men will need a good meal tonight. Were the Jews caught in the storm?"

"I'll send two scouts to find out."

∞∞∞

"They're how far ahead?" Ctesias roared the next afternoon.

"About two days. The storm didn't affect them," Zanes reported.

"How can they have such good fortune? Now we can't attack before they get to Babylon."

"The gods are against us, Ctesias. I'm going home."

Ctesias glared at Zanes. "You're giving up? After everything they've done to your family?"

"Their god is strong," Zanes protested. "Our mission has been plagued from the start. First a week's delay for the Bactrians to mourn their chieftain and now a sandstorm and another funeral. I'm going back to care for my family and business. I can't afford to follow them any longer. I need to work to support my wives and children. Otherwise, I'll end up in debt again."

The vision of plunging into debt again gave Ctesias pause, but only briefly. There was treasure to steal. Besides, his business was strong, and he had left two savvy slaves in charge of it. Either one could have run the business but might have cheated him. This way they would keep an eye on each other. "Bah. I'll do it without you," Ctesias yelled at Zanes' retreating back. "More gold for me," he muttered as his cohort disappeared in the fields of grain.

∞∞∞∞

"The Euphrates runs right through the city!" Adin exclaimed in astonishment.

"Amazing, isn't it?" Hadassah agreed. "This used to be a great seat of power, until the Babylonians rebelled and King Xerxes demolished the walls."

"Are we going into the city?"

"I'm not sure. We're meeting at the irrigation canal Ahava, which provides water for the city. Wherever it is, it will feel good to rest while abba meets with the other leaders."

The Jews waiting at the canal swelled the numbers of those already traveling with Ezra. Hadassah heard her father whisper, "Praise to Adonai," as he surveyed the masses with a wide smile.

But his joy had evaporated by the next night when he shared the family dinner silently. Miriam and Adin chattered about Babylon and seemed oblivious to their father's preoccupation.

After her sisters retired for the night, Hadassah sat with her father in front of the dying fire. "What's wrong, abba?"

"We have priests to oversee worship in the temple, but no Levites are returning. The Levites do much of the work, like stoking the fires in the altars so the priests can offer sacrifices. They organize the temple servants and serve as musicians and doorkeepers. The temple can't function properly without them. I'm talking to Adonai about what I should do. I'll attempt to sleep and hope He gives me an answer by morning. We don't have much time before we're supposed to leave."

Chapter 10

J arah impatiently brushed long brown strands of hair back under her blue headdress. Her uncle kept telling her that if she appeared to better advantage, he might receive an offer of marriage for her. *If he didn't send me to draw water like a servant, I'd look better.* She tried to shake the dirt off her long blue skirts. She could feel water seeping through the fabric on her shoulder and mud rubbing her feet under the leather sandal straps.

Jarah sighed. She had to make three trips to the well because the servants were busy preparing a feast for Iddo, the head of the Levites in Babylon. And last night her younger cousin Maya's bride price had been agreed upon. *Will I ever get to marry? My uncle's so miserly, he'll never give me a dowry, but he will require a significant bride price, claiming I'm a valuable asset. Maybe if I can escape to Jerusalem, I could find a husband.*

Jerusalem must be an improvement over Babylon. Here comes one of the town elders stumbling down the street, half out of his mind from the haoma he drank at today's sacrifice. She shook her head disapprovingly and stayed far to the other side of the street so she could avoid his wayward hands.

Worshippers of Ahura-Mazda offered sacrifices anywhere and everywhere in Persia. *If only I could participate in the temple worship at Jerusalem...*

Weeks ago the market buzzed with news about a large group, over a thousand men, returning to the land of their fathers with a priest named Ezra. Eighty years ago King Cyrus had commissioned the Jews to rebuild the temple, which had finally been completed in Darius' time. Now Ezra was returning to teach the people God's law.

It was also whispered that the Jews who returned after Cyrus' proclamation lived as they pleased, ignorant of much of the law given to Moses. And the poor who had been left in Yehud after the Babylonians destroyed the temple and deported the higher classes had even turned to idol worship.

I would also make a request if I were there—for a family of my own, a good man whose "steps are ordered by the Lord." We could have children, and I would have a family again. Aunt Pazit is such a joy and I enjoy helping her, but Uncle Barak treats me as little more than a servant. This pained her aunt, but Barak paid little attention to his wife's entreaties for her dead sister's child. Jarah was mildly surprised she was permitted to join the family for meals. Her aunt also managed to keep her well-clothed, due to Jarah's dexterity with the loom. At least she wasn't forced to wear drab cast-offs. She smiled to think how her cousins' robes would have been stretched on her ample form.

I wish Hannah could have accompanied me today. Although Hannah could manage only a small pot, Jarah enjoyed her youngest cousin's chatter, but she was in bed with a fever.

As she entered her uncle's home, she caught sight of a servant preparing vegetables with an iron knife the blacksmith had delivered yesterday. Since her aunt had been busy, she had taken him his payment. He appeared pleasant, but their encounter had been awkward. He had seemed preoccupied and stared at the darics in his large, calloused hand until she asked if it were the proper amount. His voice seemed thick and rough when he answered yes. She hoped he weren't coming down with an illness like Hannah's.

Jarah's thoughts turned back to other events of the previous day. As she had made purchases in the market, Jarah had realized she could try to return by indenturing herself to a family that *was* returning. After all, she was a free woman, not her uncle's slave. It would be difficult to leave her cousins and aunt, but there was little future for her here. Her uncle would be angry, but her aunt would understand, and if she planned carefully, he would allow her to go so he could save face.

She would find out who was going and choose one or two to approach, but she would need to hurry. They were leaving in a few days.

Jarah had pretended to examine a fruit seller's wares as she eavesdropped on the conversations buzzing around her. Intent on the gossip, she missed the fruit seller's question. Alerted by his raised brows, she stammered, "I'm sorry. I'm a bit distracted today. What did you say?"

"I asked how I could help you."

"Um, yes, well I'll take a few pomegranates." Jarah bit her lip. "I don't suppose you've heard who's travelling in the group to Yehud?"

Jarah flushed under the farmer's searching gaze as she handed him a daric and chose some pomegranates.

"I've heard of a few—Hashabiah's family, Sherebiah's family. Since Ezra sent a message asking for Levites to join the group, over thirty men have decided to go. I'd wager a few more are thinking on it."

"Thank you. You've been very helpful." She knew one of the women in Sherebiah's family. Avital had purchased several pieces of cloth from Jarah this year. Jarah would speak with her first.

She hurried through the dusty streets to the home Avital shared with her husband and four children. The mud-brick dwelling was surrounded by a small courtyard full of pistachio trees and vegetables. Jarah passed through a wall higher than her head and found the mistress of the house seated on a bench pounding barley into flour with a mortar and pestle.

"Shalom," Jarah greeted Avital.

"Shalom, Jarah. It's good to see you, especially today. Forgive me for grinding while we catch up," Avital answered. "I have more grain to grind than I can possibly get through. My sister is coming tomorrow to help me."

Jarah rejoiced at the ease of turning this conversation towards the coming journey. "I suppose you're preparing for the trek back to Yehud?"

"Word travels fast. Yes, my husband wants to return with his father and brothers. Our children are old enough to undertake the journey, so we're going." Avital sighed.

"No one from your family's going, are they?" Jarah asked gently.

"No." Avital tried to smile. "But my place is with my husband's family, of course."

"Yes." Jarah briefly considered the pain of separating from her loved ones, but plunged ahead. "Would you like some company? I'd like to go. Maybe I could help with cooking and gathering fuel and other tasks."

Avital beamed. "I'd like that more than I could say. Keeping track of my younger two might present a challenge. I'll talk to my husband and see what he says. Can you come back tomorrow?"

"Absolutely." Jarah had left with a song in her heart.

Now it was time to discover her destiny with a second trip to Avital's house. After depositing the water pots in the kitchen, she hurried off before she was given more chores.

Her mind buzzed with possibilities and prayers as she hurried the short distance to Avital's home. "Shalom, Avital."

"Shalom," Avital replied curtly.

Jarah's stomach fluttered. She waited, but Avital remained silent.

"So, what did your husband think about my accompanying you?"

"He thinks you should have the blessing of your uncle."

Jarah gulped. "So the answer's 'no.'"

"Exactly. And I don't appreciate the position you put me in. Elrad happened to see your uncle and mention the journey. Let's just say your uncle wasn't pleased."

"I'm sorry, Avital. It wasn't my intention to cause any problems for your family."

"You know how powerful your uncle is in Casiphia. It's a good thing we're leaving now that he thinks we've crossed him." Avital softened a little. "Take care, Jarah."

Crushed, Jarah turned away. She'd never be able to join the group now, and her uncle would make life harder. She had better stay out of his sight for a while. At least tonight he'd be busy with important visitors.

∞∞∞∞

That evening Jarah helped her cousin Naomi serve Iddo, his four sons, her uncle, and his only son, Hur. After the women cleared away the remnants of the stew and fruit, the men remained to talk. As Jarah finished and went to check on Hannah, Naomi beckoned her to the curtained doorway where she'd been listening. Jarah crept up the wall toward her cousin and identified Iddo's voice.

"Many of those remaining here in Persia are helping our brothers as they return to Jerusalem with Ezra. Not all gifts are strictly gold and silver or precious wares. She'd be a good addition to those returning to Yehud. I've seen how hard she works. My wife certainly appreciates the fine cloth she weaves."

Jarah looked at Naomi in puzzlement, but Naomi put a finger to her lips.

"I'll think on it, Iddo. Perhaps it is something I could do to help the cause, if she's not averse to going. I wouldn't want to force her. After all, her family is here, and my wife is quite fond of her."

Slowly it dawned on Jarah that these men were discussing *her*. But why? Had Iddo heard of her attempt to return with Avital's family? Maybe Ezra wanted cloth makers to return with the Levites in order to decorate the temple in Jerusalem. She tried to picture the temple from the descriptions she had heard. A heavy curtain separated the holy of holies from the main part of the temple. There were probably other drapes too, and the priests' garments. Her dream of offering a sacrifice in the temple could still come true!

She slipped away from the door to beseech Adonai for his favor, leaving Naomi to continue her eavesdropping. As she prayed, a portion of the Writings came to her mind: "For a day in your courts is better than a thousand outside. I would rather stand at the threshold of the house of my God than dwell in the tents of wickedness."

Chapter 11

T he next morning Jarah moved to her loom early. If her uncle did allow her to leave, she wanted to finish this last span of linen cloth. Maybe her aunt would allow her to keep it in her new life, but even if she had another purpose for it, Jarah wanted to complete it. Hannah reclined on a nearby cushion.

"Are you feeling better?"

"Yes, not as hot as yesterday," Hannah said. "Em made me some broth."

"How about if I sing for you?"

"I'd like that."

So Jarah began a joyful psalm, and soon Hannah was humming along.

The blacksmith paused before knocking on the door, transfixed by the melody. The song reminded him of his younger sister Elizabeth. She had died three years ago in childbirth, a beautiful but delicate woman. The babe died with her. He had thought the grief would gut him, but now he could think of her without the intense pain. Her young husband didn't seem as stricken as Oren and soon remarried. Oren questioned if the fellow even remembered his sister, but as long as he lived, his sister's saucy laugh and merry singing would ring in his memory, even as he traveled to a foreign place, with a new bride.

Will there be good news about Jarah? Jarah reminds me of my sister. I'm not sure why. She's plain, unlike Liza. And I've never spoken with her, except for yesterday.

His reveries ended as a dark-skinned servant child opened the door with a flourish.

"Jarah, your uncle wishes to speak with you in the anteroom," her aunt announced, entering the room. "Here, straighten your skirt and hair, dear." Pazit always fussed with Jarah's appearance before she faced her uncle, so this was nothing unusual, but Pazit's beaming smile reassured Jarah. "Hannah, you stay here."

Hannah remained contentedly on her cushions, knowing she would hear the entire conversation through the wide arched doorways. She flashed Jarah an impish smile.

When the women bustled into the anteroom, Jarah noticed the blacksmith was present again. He looked pale and serious. Jarah tried to assess her uncle's mood. He seemed solemn too.

"Jarah, we have a matter of importance to discuss. Oren would like to ask you a question."

So that's the blacksmith's name. She turned towards him.

He cleared his throat a bit nervously. "Would you like to return to Yehud with me?"

"Yes, I would."

Barak sucked in a noisy breath, but Pazit quickly headed off any comment by taking his arm and leaving with a parting of, "You'll have lots to discuss. Come see me when you're done, Jarah."

Oren sagged and quickly sat down on a bench by the wall. Jarah remained standing. "Are you sure you don't need more time to think about it? Not that we have much time..." he stumbled to a stop, his face reddening.

"I would like to worship at the Most High's temple," Jarah responded.

Oren looked a bit puzzled and mumbled, "I guess that's about the best I could hope for."

"I'll only bring what I can carry, and I'll serve you well," Jarah assured him, trying to ease his discomfort.

Now Oren's eyebrows nearly met in the middle. He com-

43

posed himself. "We'll need more than you can carry. Don't leave anything useful behind. I'm sure your aunt will give you some type of bridal gift."

Jarah's head snapped up. "What?" Her face flooded with color.

"What exactly did the question I asked mean to you?" he asked softly.

"I...I...thought I was traveling with you to Jerusalem to sew for the temple, as your indentured servant."

"Where did you get that idea?" Oren asked, a smile beginning.

"I . . . heard a little of the conversation last night when Iddo was speaking to my uncle. I'm known for weaving cloth, and they were talking about my being a good addition for the group going back." Jarah blushed deeply. The headman hadn't meant as a worker; he'd meant as a wife!

Oren sobered and said gently, "That's not what I meant, Jarah. Let me make myself clear. I won't hold you to your first answer, and you can take an evening to think about it. Will you become my wife this week and travel to Yehud with me? My family owns a house in Gibeon. It's about a day's walk from Jerusalem. I'm not sure we'll be able to take possession of it immediately, but we can survive with my blacksmithing trade, and your skill as a weaver could help us too."

Jarah covered her face with her hands while Oren waited, not certain whether to leave or stay. First he heard giggles, followed by laughter. "I'm such a fool," Jarah gasped, trying to regain her composure. "Are you sure you want to marry me?"

Oren nodded, "More sure than before."

"How can that be?"

"I miss laughter. There isn't much where I live. I also know you're not proud. A lot of women would be mortified and wouldn't see anything funny in the situation." He grinned. "You're very attractive when you're laughing."

"I do laugh a lot. My uncle says I should be more serious."

"Forget about your uncle. I'm about to become the man in your life...I hope."

"I thought you were married! You're always part of a group of women and men. I've even seen you carrying a little boy."

"He's my nephew. I live with my two brothers and their families near our blacksmith shop. All twelve of us cram into two small houses in the courtyard. That's why I'm always part of a crowd. I should let you know, I don't have much. We're all rather poor. It's the reason I'm marrying older than most."

"You realize I'm twenty-two?"

"I knew you were a little older." Noticing a shade of apprehension on her face, Oren added, "It's not because you're lacking, Jarah. I know of two men who approached your uncle about you in the last five years, but your uncle required a high bride price and offered little dowry. They felt they needed a better start, so they found brides whose parents were willing to help set up their housekeeping without taking all their silver."

"But if you don't have the bride price, why did my uncle accept your offer?"

"Iddo spoke with him about the sacrifices the sons of Israel are making to send gifts back to Jerusalem with Ezra."

My uncle didn't want to part with his gold or silver, but he's willing to send me.

"He doesn't know your true worth, Jarah."

Jarah studied Oren. He seemed kind. He was strong. He valued family. "I don't need an evening to consider an answer, Oren. I'd still like to go with you. I'd rather be a wife than an indentured servant any day!" she added with a glint of humor in her eyes.

After arranging a meeting for the following morning to talk about gathering the necessities for their journey and to choose a wedding day, they parted.

Out on the dusty street, Oren broke into a huge grin. "Thank you, Jehovah-Jireh, for you have provided." His thoughts went back to the events of the week which had put him on this path.

Chapter 12

Yesterday Oren had awakened with the knowledge that he had to leave Babylon and return to the land of his forefathers. He had listened to Iddo, the Levites' chief, when he had called the people to the marketplace and announced, "Ezra has personally asked for more Levites to return to Yehud to serve in the temple."

"Do you want to go, Oren?" his brother Jehu had asked as they walked back to the blacksmith's shed where Dan still labored.

"I don't want to leave you and Dan without enough help. We need to make and repair enough tools and weapons to feed our family," Oren replied.

"You've sacrificed having your own family to help me and Dan provide for our families. We haven't been able to figure out a way to pay the bride price and support more mouths. This could be your chance, Oren. Our family owned property in Yehud. You can go claim it."

"But you won't be able to operate the forge for as many hours if I leave," Oren protested.

"My son has gained eleven summers and has grown like a reed these last few moons. We can train him to keep the heat at the right level. Soon he'll be strong enough to shape simple iron tools. Oren, both Dan and I married long before your age. We appreciate your pitching in to help us, but it would be selfish to keep you any longer if you want to take this opportunity."

As Oren spelled Dan in the hot shed, he considered his options. *If I return to Yehud, there will be an inheritance waiting--my family's property in Gibeon, not far from Jerusalem. We were dragged into captivity by Nebuchadnezzar a century and a half ago, but since we received the land from Adonai it belongs to us forever. We've learned at bet 'amma that the Lord might punish idolatry and scatter us, but He always keeps his promises.*

The problem lay in how he could survive until he reached Yehud. He possessed only a piece of silver and a few coins along with his clothes. At least he wouldn't be burdened with a large load. His brothers' wives would give him food for the journey. Then he thought of their sparse supplies. Maybe they could spare him enough for a couple of weeks. He might even need to indenture himself to a fellow Jew who could use his skills and strength on the journey. He would consult Iddo.

Iddo listened carefully as Oren told him his plan. Stroking his graying beard, he did not answer quickly. "No man should return to the land of his forefathers as an indentured servant," he finally pronounced. "Our community is gathering funds for the temple and the sacrifices. We will support your return. Your skills as a blacksmith will be invaluable."

He sank into contemplation while Oren waited respectfully. "Oren, the Lord is impressing on me that you need to take a wife with you. Do you have the bride's price?"

"I only have one piece of silver, and I don't have much to offer her right now except a long, uncomfortable journey."

"But there's a home waiting for you at the end of the road."

"Yes, but I don't know what condition it's in."

"The Lord will prepare your way just as he prepared Eleazar's when he sought a wife for Isaac. Rebekah also undertook a long trek to a new land," Iddo said kindly. "Is there a particular girl?"

Oren swallowed. "I . . . er . . . favor Barak's girls, though I don't know any of them well."

Iddo closed his eyes and resumed stroking his beard. "There are five damsels in his house, all appealing. They're not accustomed to hardship and at least one has already married. Barak will expect a good price for his remaining daughters." His eyes snapped open. "He's also cared for his niece for several years. The girl's name is Jarah, a little older. Go and see if she pleases you. If she does, I'll speak to Barak on your behalf."

Oren returned to the forge and told his brothers about the conversation. Dan and Jehu exchanged looks, and Jehu went to the table where small finished pieces lay. "The Most High must be smiling down on you today. Barak's wife ordered this kitchen knife. Why don't you deliver it and collect payment instead of waiting for a servant to come for it?"

Oren had nervously gathered the knife and made his way to Barak's imposing compound. He lived on a huge tract of land with his two brothers. Each of the three families inhabited a large home built of kilned brick and painted a different color. Their courtyards fronted the main road, but joined each other with elegant gates. Oren liked walking by because he could smell the fragrant citrus and roses. The home's interior had been impressive too. The anteroom where he had waited for Jarah to pay him was painted with murals of blue and green birds.

He had liked the kind yet direct manner of the tall, big-boned woman and had returned to Iddo and told him she would make a worthy wife. Iddo had spoken to Barak last night. And now Jarah had agreed!

When he entered the courtyard where his brothers were laboring, they slapped him on the back. "From the looks of you, you were successful. Congratulations!" his eldest brother Jehu greeted him. Looking over at Dan, he added, "We have something for you out in the stable."

As they entered the musty stable, the scent of donkeys assailed Oren. Their ancient donkey, a gray mare, and her foal lived here among an assortment of harnesses and blankets. "We're giving you the mare since you'll need a beast for your journey," Dan said.

Oren was shocked. "But she does all the work around here. Old Joe's not good for much, and the foal's too young."

"Joe will probably last until the foal's old enough to mate, so we should always have two donkeys. We'll manage," Jehu said.

"You've earned her," Dan added. "You've been helping us since you were a boy, and we never gave you much beyond your keep."

"Granted you do eat a lot," Jehu said with a grin. "Always have."

Oren swallowed a lump in his throat. "Thank you. I know it will be hard on the two of you for a while," Oren said regretfully. "But I figured it was leave now or never. Abe's helping out with errands and soon he'll be ready to train."

"It's the right time, Oren. If Abe and our other sons turn out to be half the worker you are, we'll double our business by the time they're ready to marry. We're just sorry you had to wait this long. Never realized you were interested," Dan said.

"Not until lately. But Jarah's uncle wasn't ready to part with her any earlier either," Oren said with a wry smile. "I think it's been hard on her. She didn't think anyone wanted her."

"You treat her good, and she'll be glad she had to wait around for you." Jehu slapped him on the back. "Need any pointers?"

Jarah composed herself and went to the kitchen to speak with her aunt. She was relieved her uncle had left for the day. *I think he expected me to reject Oren's proposal. He only allowed the offer to appease Iddo and make it look like he supports the returning Jews.*

Her aunt encompassed her in a hug. "He seems like a good man, Jarah. I am *so* happy for you." Pazit wiped tears from her eyes as they sat on benches at the table. "Now we must decide what you should take with you. We don't have much time. You'll need food--barley for bread, figs, dates. I'm going to give you Sheba so you'll always have a little milk. You'll need something to sleep on, some cooking pots, water jugs. What else? You've always been the sensible one. I'm not sure how we'll manage without you." Pazit gave her another hug as she rose. "Let's inspect the trunk full of cloth. You'll need something nice to wear for your marriage. You can save it for your best dress. How many dresses do you have now, dear? Enough for a long, dusty trip?"

Jarah struggled to keep up with her aunt's questions. "I have two good dresses, and two really old ones fine for travelling."

"When will the wedding be? I need to have a sheep prepared for the guests."

"I was thinking in two days."

Pazit's hand flew to her chest. "That doesn't give us much time, but we'll manage. I want to send a gift to the temple, and I have this chest full of cloth, so I'll give as much as you can carry. We'll wrap it in goatskin that you can use for tenting."

"Thank you, Auntie."

"You have blessed this house from the moment you arrived at ten years old, Jarah. I'm sorry I can't do more for you." She placed one hand on Jarah's shoulder and wiped her eyes with the other. "I remember my *softa* telling me about Jerusalem and the temple. Her mother told her about visiting the temple for Passover. They both believed our family would return one day. Softa said the Most High promised to bring some of us back, and her family would be included. You are the one the Most High has chosen. I'm thankful to see her prophecy come true."

Pazit drew a long piece of scarlet cloth from the leather trunk. "I was saving this for a special occasion. Today is the day. Please take it to the temple as an offering from your old aunt. And this blue one is for you."

Jarah recognized a piece of cloth she had woven years ago and her aunt had dyed a deep sky blue.

"I was saving it for your wedding dress, but you'll be married quickly, and there's so much to be done..." Pazit's voice trailed off.

"I don't need a new dress. I'm thankful God provided the groom. I've been waiting you know." Jarah and her aunt laughed.

∞∞∞

Two days of intense preparation disappeared as fast as dew before the scorching sun. The sacred vows were exchanged by candlelight beneath a night sky sparkling with stars. Warmed by fires, the families celebrated in Barak's courtyard, and the overflow of guests spilled through the open gates into his brother's courtyard. While the revelers danced, Oren escorted his new wife to their bridal chamber. Iddo had arranged for them to use one of Sherebiah's small but luxurious homes since their clan had already gathered at the canal. "May your marriage be blessed with long life and many sons," he said, pressing a pouch of silver pieces into Oren's hands.

As the couple left, Pazit told them, "We'll pack your supplies and gifts. Come early the morning you're leaving to see that the donkey is loaded to your liking, but that's all. Focus on each other for these two precious nights."

Chapter 13

Hadassah plodded along with the women of the caravan, who walked to the side to avoid the grit kicked up by the donkeys and camels. Her father rode a light-colored donkey near the head of the column. Most of the men followed within the next half parasang, leading beasts laden with baggage. A score of camels interspersed throughout the caravan carried treasure for the temple. The goats and sheep straggled behind with their herders and several lookouts as the rear guard.

So far the journey had been a safe one. The God of Israel had answered the prayers they had offered as they fasted beside the river. Her father had hesitated to request soldiers' protection, and the king had not offered, so the rich caravan travelled as a tightly woven group rather than strung out like beads on a necklace. The Almighty had also protected them from the fierce sandstorms of the region.

Hadassah's thoughts dwelt in the past, remembering Jedid-iah, her husband of three years. How she wished she had borne a son resembling him. She longed to see his bushy eyebrows and clear brown eyes. Eventually their son would have gained the muscle of his father and taken care of his mother. But there was no son, nor daughter, just memory.

Hadassah paused to sip water from the goatskin she carried and shook the memories from her mind. She looked around for her youngest sister, Adin, to ensure her well-being. Adin was talking and laughing with other girls her age.

I wonder how Esther is managing without me. Her maid can help her dress until a replacement can be trained, but the queen was more like family than my mistress. Although she's not really the queen any more, that's the way I'll always think of her.

She had never noticed King Artaxerxes' attention before Esther's revelation, but afterwards she had surreptitiously watched him as he watched her. His interest had alarmed her. Neither she nor the queen wanted her to be forced into the harem. Esther had suffered much, although she had occupied the chief position in the harem for years. Artaxerxes still protected his adoptive mother and allowed her to retain the rooms she had resided in for twenty years.

Hadassah clearly remembered the anguish of her mother Rachel when news came that the queen's adopted son, Sparamizes, had been poisoned. Rachel, pregnant and nauseated, had cried for days, and Ezra had stayed home to supervise his daughters and comfort his wife.

One night she lay awake listening to her mother weeping and overheard her parents' conversation. "But why?" Rachel had cried to her husband. "She only had two sons, and now one is dead. She will never have another child to comfort her."

"The Most High's ways are not our ways," Ezra had replied. His words seemed to lack comfort, for her mother had cried harder.

Now she understood how her mother felt. *Why does the Almighty allow untimely deaths? An old person, full of years, should go to his reward. But not a man in his prime, nor a little boy. Is He actually in control? Doesn't He care?*

Sparamizes' murder had probably been the worst experience of Esther's life in the harem, but the pain hadn't ended there. Eventually Xerxes had been murdered by Artabanus, his chief bodyguard. Although her relationship with Xerxes had risen and fallen over the years, Esther had been truly saddened by her husband's violent end and had watched in horror as Darius, the prince next in line for the throne, had been accused and executed for his father's death.

Artabanus had appointed himself regent until Artaxerxes was older. Artaxerxes, however, had inherited his father's temper and simply bided his time until he surprised Artabanus with a taste of his own sword. At thirteen, Artaxerxes became king and gladly abandoned himself to royal profligacy. His personal decisions had burdened Esther, but, with the help of his official council, he ruled his kingdom well.

Esther had been well cared for physically, but her life was marred by the violent deaths of her loved ones. *Why does she continue to develop deep relationships? She's lost almost everyone she loves, if not through murder, then because she insists on acting in their best interests. That's why I'm on this journey instead of serving her in the palace. She wanted me to be free, and I'm grateful.* The gratitude was a mere stirring, but Hadassah was relieved to feel *something. . .*

Tired of her own company, Hadassah studied her fellow bedraggled travelers. Most of the women had already formed groups. A few of the mothers with young children had banded together for encouragement and help in towing their youngsters. As they laughed and chattered with each other, the maidens like Adin pitched in and played with or carried little ones. Only a couple of women walked alone. One was a woman of Hadassah's age, a new bride, who drifted dreamily among the other knots of women, nodding and humming. The other was a petite woman who might have been pretty if she hadn't been stomping along with an angry frown. Hadassah decided to catch up to the new bride.

"Shalom. My name is Hadassah."

The new bride startled and blushed. "My name's Jarah. Sorry I didn't see you there. I've only been married a little while." She paused. "Two moons ago I feared my chance had passed and I'd never marry. I'm still savoring the joy of it." Her radiant face made Hadassah's heart ache, and Hadassah fervently hoped Jarah wouldn't ask about her husband.

"You're traveling with your father and sisters, aren't you?" Jarah continued. "How many sisters do you have?"

"There are four of us. I'm the eldest, but fortunately even the youngest is able to look after herself. We all help with setting up camp and cooking. My sister's husband does the heavy lifting. Is it just you and your husband, or are you traveling with relatives?"

"It's just the two of us. I'm glad. There's a little more privacy. We don't have to share a tent at least," Jarah joked. "It does make the cooking and water carrying a bit difficult, but Oren's been lugging the wood and starting the fire, so I manage."

Hadassah wanted to pursue her companion's comment about thinking she would never marry, but decided she didn't know her well enough. The two walked in companionable silence until the party halted for the evening meal.

∞∞∞

The next morning Jarah found Hadassah in the crowd. "Want some company today?" she queried.

"I'd love it," Hadassah answered.

As the caravan wound through the sparse, rocky land, Hadassah commented, "The cloth of your dress is very fine. I used to wait on the queen, and her court wore linen like yours."

"I'm a weaver, and this cloth is fine, but the dress is quite old. If you look closely, you'll see it's been mended many times. Plus it's a drab dust color. I figured it's perfect for this journey." Jarah asked with a grimace, "Does the grit bother you? It's driving me crazy! There's not enough water to bathe. I always feel dirty and unkempt, which isn't the way I imagined welcoming a husband to my bed."

A little startled by the last revelation, Hadassah tried to comfort her new friend. "My father says we'll reach an oasis in a few days. There will be plenty of water." Hadassah looked down at her filthy, sandal-clad feet. "And yes, I miss bathing too. There were baths at the palace, and I went with the queen nearly every day. The dirt in the streets of Susa is bad, but out here I can taste the dust. Even when I drink, there seems to be dust in the water. I can't wait until we get to Jerusalem and settle into a home."

"Why are you going to Jerusalem? It sounds like you had a great position with the queen."

Hadassah smiled at her new friend's bluntness. "In the palace, we measured our words. There always seemed to be a plot afoot, an assassination planned. Treason suspects were executed swiftly, so no one wanted to be misunderstood. But here I guess I can speak freely."

Yet habits were hard to break, and she hesitated until Jarah prompted, "So?"

"King Artaxerxes wanted to add me to his harem. Queen Esther and I didn't think that was best for me."

Jarah gasped and looked at her in horror, at a loss for words.

Hadassah shrugged. "Why are you going to Jerusalem?"

Regrouping, Jarah gulped. "And I believed my story was dramatic! I'll want to hear more eventually. Imagine…wanted by the king! As for me, it began simply. I wanted to give an offering in the temple and have a new life, so I tried to go with a family I know. Then Oren asked me to go. I thought he meant as a servant for the journey, but he meant as his wife." Jarah's dark eyes sparkled with humor.

Hadassah tried to digest the information. "Why did you think he wanted you to go as a servant?"

"That would have been my position with the other family. Plus Iddo, the leader of the Levites, was eating with my uncle, and I overheard them discussing my weaving skills. When Oren showed up asking me to return, I put everything together and came up with the wrong conclusion entirely." Jarah laughed. "I assumed he was married because I would see him with his nephews and nieces. You should have seen his face when I answered 'yes' right away, with none of the coyness or games of young women."

Hadassah's lips curved into a smile as she pictured the mix-up.

"I'm a direct person anyway, so I guess it was best he knew from the beginning."

"I like your directness. It's refreshing. In the palace, there's a lot of flattery and pretense. I like talking with someone who says what she thinks."

"Sounds like all that plotting would make a woman think before speaking."

"Yes, always a scheme against someone, a servant, a concubine, a member of the royal family. And many of them succeed. It gets messy. The night King Xerxes was murdered, I helped Queen Esther keep watch all night. She was afraid there would be more bloodshed. I'm not going to miss all the intrigue."

A slight sadness in Hadassah's tone alerted Jarah that she would miss other aspects of palace life. She took her new friend's arm.

"My grandmother used to tell me stories about the temple. She had learned them from her grandmother. How it glowed in the sun's light due to all the gold. The rich reds of the tapestries. I could almost feel them, Hadassah! I want to make new ones."

"So your grandmother's grandmother lived in Yehud when the Babylonians destroyed the city?"

"Yes. She and my grandfather survived the brutal trip to Babylon. One of their children didn't make it. Two others were left behind. They never found out what happened to them. They were able to have one more child—my great grandmother.

"My grandmother and grandfather were planning to return with Zerubbabel, but his father became crippled. They stayed behind to care for him. My softa Sarah always told me to return if I had the opportunity.

"My uncle found out about my first attempt to join this group and didn't give his blessing. He's a powerful man in our community, and they wouldn't dare cross him. I wasn't going to be able to come, but a few days before everyone left Oren asked me to join him as his wife. Funny thing is, there was some kind of accident, and Avital's family stayed behind." Jarah's voice held a hint of awe. "Look how the Almighty worked on my behalf."

Maybe He'll work on mine, too.

Chapter 14

As men positioned tents in tight formation and women tended cooking fires, Hadassah stiffened at the sounds of raised voices a few fires beyond hers.

"I hate this trip. My feet hurt. My back hurts. I hate the dust," a woman complained.

A man's voice rumbled in answer, but Hadassah couldn't make out the words.

"Washing my feet hardly begins to help." The woman sounded infuriated. "Cook your own meal. I'm going to lie down."

When Hadassah walked through the cooking fires later that evening to fetch a jug of water, she looked for the site of the argument. Two men sat morosely at their fire, trying to eat the charred remains of their supper. "She'll come around, Ariel. She has to. Maybe if you were more firm with her..."

So the husband of the angry woman was Ariel. Maybe she could ease the situation tomorrow by speaking with his wife.

∞ ∞ ∞

When Jarah joined her the next morning, Hadassah asked if she knew the wife of Ariel. "I should know who she is, but I've been...distracted."

Jarah scanned the chattering girls and the matrons guiding their children. "I don't see her right now. Here, come off to the side. I'll pretend to adjust my sandal, and we'll find her if she's coming along behind. I imagine you heard their fight too?"

"Just her side of it. I'm hoping I can help her a little so she's not miserable tonight."

"You're going to have quite the job," Jarah said, as the crowd passed by and revealed a woman retching into the bushes behind the convoy. "That's Naama, wife of Ariel."

"I see," Hadassah said slowly. "This is going to be more challenging than I imagined."

"Do you want me to come with you?"

"I'd appreciate it."

When Naama looked up from her sickness, Hadassah offered her a damp cloth. "Maybe this will help. Would you like a sip of water?"

The girl dabbed her colorless face with the cool cloth. "I'm afraid to put anything else in my stomach. I'll pass on the water for now," she answered faintly.

Hadassah pitied her. "How long have you been ill?"

"A few weeks. It started just after Ariel dragged me into this caravan."

Jarah felt the girl's forehead. "You're not warm." She and Hadassah exchanged a long look, pregnant with meaning.

Naama sighed. "Yes, I know I'm expecting. My softa was the royal mid-wife. My mother and I are rug weavers, but I grew up around discussions of pregnancy and delivery. Excuse me." She turned and threw up again, then patted her face with the cloth. Hadassah and Jarah urged her to rest in their shadows.

After the livestock and their herders rumbled by, Naama said, "I feel a little better now. I'm sick a few times every morning, but it passes. I'm so tired, though. All this walking! And the dust! Why does a man pick the worst possible time to move his wife hundreds of parasangs away from her family to a place he's never even seen?"

Hadassah looked toward the horizon and fought for control. If only this girl understood how much she had—a husband, and a child on the way!

Jarah looked at her curiously, but when Hadassah said nothing, she soothed Naama, "I know you're wishing for your softa and em right now, but we'll do the best we can for you. We'd better catch up, or we might fall prey to bandits."

Naama rose with Jarah's help but muttered, "It would serve Ariel right if I were carried off. Maybe he'd realize what he's done."

The women soon passed the animals and joined the rest of the women. Since neither Hadassah nor Naama spoke, Jarah began to chatter about her aunt and uncle's family. Soon Naama laughed, and even Hadassah began smiling about the family's antics.

∞∞∞∞

Jarah didn't hear any yelling that evening in the camp. But why had Hadassah withdrawn from Naama when it was her idea to befriend her in the first place?

∞∞∞∞

The next morning Jarah looked for Hadassah as soon as she and Oren had packed their goat's hair tent, bedding, and camp pottery onto their gray donkey. After the caravan started moving west, Jarah suggested, "Let's see how Naama is doing today."

Hadassah hesitated but said, "Yes, that's a good idea."

The friends found Naama huddled behind a scrubby bush, just as sick as the day before.

This is going to be a long journey, Jarah thought. Fortunately, the morning sickness passed, and Naama was able to walk slowly, keeping ahead of the herded animals whose smell made her feel more ill. By afternoon, she was joking with an acerbic wit in response to Jarah's conversation. Hadassah kept quiet, and eventually went to walk with her sisters Miriam and Rebekah.

∞∞∞

Early the next morning Jarah found Hadassah. She noticed the dark circles beneath her eyes. "What's wrong, friend?"

"I'm okay. Let's check on Naama."

Jarah put a hand on her arm to stop her. "Right now I'm more concerned about you. She'll be all right for a little while. There's precious little we can do for her while she's sick."

Hadassah looked away.

Jarah persisted, "We haven't known each other long, but one thing you'll learn about me is I'm persistent. You can tell me now, or I'll keep pestering you with the same question until I get an answer." She gestured toward the desert. "There's nowhere to hide." Her voice softened. "Please tell me, Hadassah. I know I probably can't help you, but it might make you feel better if you talk about it."

Hadassah sighed. "I know Naama's miserable because she's sick, but she has *everything, everything,* Jarah, and she doesn't even know it. All she does is complain. I would give *anything* to have my Jedidiah back or to have his baby growing within me, but I have nothing. I feel terrible because I know I shouldn't be angry with her, but I am." She looked away in shame. "There, now you know. I expect you'll walk with someone else."

"Why would I walk with someone else because you're human, Hadassah? I didn't know about your husband. I've been too wrapped up in myself. I'm sorry. When did he die?"

"About four moons ago, of a fever. He didn't know me the last few days."

Jarah enfolded her in a hug as Hadassah began to cry.

Their previous conversations made sense to Jarah now. "And the king was waiting before taking you into the harem, but you're escaping to Yehud."

"Yes, I can take care of my father there."

"Oh Hadassah. The idea of losing Oren...how long were you

61

married?"

"Three years. I should have had a child by now. Watching Naama is difficult. I don't think she wants her baby."

"She's barely a woman. We're older, Hadassah. We know what's important."

"I know. I keep telling myself she's my youngest sister's age. I feel awful that I resent her, but I can't seem to stop those feelings."

The two walked in silence for a while. "I feel like I should see how Naama's doing," Jarah said. "I'll come find you when I know she'll be okay on her own."

"I'm coming too."

"You don't need to do that."

"Yes, I do. I'm a better person than my jealousy. Let's go."

Mounted on his ebony stallion, Ctesias watched the lone woman huddled in the dirt. He was about to swoop down on her when a sharp-eyed Bedouin raised his hand and said "Wait."

To Ctesias' delight, two other women emerged from the dust trailing the herd of animals.

"Don't make any noise. It'll scare those Jews spitless when their women disappear."

He gave the signal and led the band down a slight rise, cutting across its face to separate the women from their caravan. But as he passed a rocky outcropping, his horse, Jasper, shied and bolted directly up the rise, away from the women. Ctesias struggled to keep his seat on the spooked animal. When the stallion finally stopped, thoroughly winded, he was surprised to find his men following him.

"What about the women?" he roared as they caught up.

"We left the boy to watch. It looked like you might need help," explained his second-in-command.

"You stay here until this beast recovers. Then meet us behind the caravan," Ctesias said curtly. He switched mounts with his lieutenant and loped back toward the women.

Naama had fallen far behind the animals by the time Jarah and Hadassah found her. "It's worse this morning," she told them.

Hadassah watched as the last animals disappeared from her view in a cloud of dust. "We'll help you, but we have to catch up. The lookouts saw signs of horsemen behind us yesterday."

"Why didn't your father ask for soldiers to accompany us?" Jarah asked.

"He didn't want King Artaxerxes to think the One True God couldn't protect us."

"It would be better than all this worry about being attacked," Naama grumbled as she rose from the ground and took Jarah's arm. Hadassah grasped Naama's other arm, and the two older women propelled their younger charge along.

"Thank you for all the help," Naama said as they caught up with the animals.

"Have you told your husband yet?" Jarah asked.

"No."

"I think he may have figured it out," Hadassah said.

"No, men are fools about these things."

Hadassah gestured toward a horseman fast approaching them. It looked like he had been on guard duty, but now he was coming toward them at a quick trot.

"That *is* Ariel," Naama acknowledged, squinting into the distance. "Someone loaned him a horse, so he could be a guard."

As the horseman drew up, he slid off his mount. "Naama, are you okay?" he asked in a worried voice.

"I don't feel too well." She dropped the arms of her friends and motioned for them to go ahead. "But I'll be fine. I have news for you."

As Jarah and Hadassah walked out of earshot, Hadassah heard an excited shout from Ariel. She felt a twinge of envy.

Ctesias studied the dust behind the caravan. "How long ago did they disappear?"

"Awhile. Right after your mount saw that serpent, the women started walking. A man on a horse joined them, just as they caught up to the herd."

"Another attempt foiled." Ctesias cursed by the gods. "All because of a snake!"

Naama caught up to her two friends after the noon meal. Color had returned to her face, along with a peace they had never seen.

"Ariel sounded happy," Jarah commented.

"Yes. He offered to let me ride our donkey, but the thought of the up-and-down motion made me queasy just to think of it. It was kind of him, though. I know he was tired after scouting, and he would have been walking with a large load if I took him up on his offer."

"I realized this morning I may have a root that will ease the morning sickness," Jarah offered. "If you boil a piece of ginger root in water and drink it, you may feel better. I'll get it from my bag when we stop for the night and bring it to your fire, so you can try it tomorrow. If that doesn't work, we'll ask the other women for some advice."

"Thank you, Jarah. Things are looking up for me today." Naama's smile lit her face and revealed dimples her friends had never seen.

Chapter 15

Hadassah slogged along by herself through the loose sand. *Jedidiah died almost five moons ago. Why couldn't I have a child who would be keeping part of him alive? He could have Jedidiah's dimple. Or our daughter could have his brown eyes.*

"How long have you been here?" Hadassah asked when she finally noticed Jarah walking alongside her.

"Since we crested that last low hill. I couldn't figure out what to say. You look so sad."

Hadassah glanced behind at the hill all the travelers had traversed. Now the herds and their dust clogged the horizon. When she didn't respond, Jarah continued, "Are you thinking of Jedidiah?"

"Yes, and what our children might have looked like." The two trudged along in silence as the day grew hot. "Have you ever felt Adonai has forgotten you?"

"I was an orphan. I was convinced Adonai didn't care about me, but one day I heard something amazing at the *bet 'amma*. 'Behold I have inscribed you on the palms of my hands.' When I heard those words, I wasn't sure I could believe them, but I hoped it was true. I use my hands to weave, so I'm always mindful of them. Right before those words Adonai promised: 'I will not forget you.' The priest was reading from the prophet Isaiah about how we would be delivered from those who conquered us and would return to our land. And look! Now we're returning. I'm returning."

Jarah considered the rocky vista before them. "I think if part of the promise is true, all of it must be. Adonai didn't forget me while I lived with my uncle. He had me on his mind, even though I didn't think he heard my prayers. I couldn't marry and settle down like I wanted because then I wouldn't be returning with his people as Oren's wife."

Hadassah considered Jarah's words. She wouldn't be returning either if Jedidiah had lived. She would never have seen her father or sisters again. "You think God keeps a poor widow's name on his hand as a constant reminder?"

"I do. He hasn't forgotten you."

∞∞∞

Two moons had passed since Judith's journey to see her family. She still missed the jangle of the bracelets Benjamin had given her after a successful grape harvest. She told him she lost them during her visit home, which was true enough. She had traded them for two doves. To make up for the smallness of her gift, she had climbed to the highest hill of sacrifice. Today she was happy, and hopeful Moloch had heard, for she had felt movement like a moth's flutter. She was sure it was the baby, but she would clean their rooms quickly this morning and take her grain over to Tova's home to grind, so she could ask her friend.

Tova already appeared uncomfortable and hot though the fields still sipped the morning dew. Her stomach made the task of grinding nearly impossible. It was difficult for her to squat because she was off-balance. Judith nearly laughed when she entered the one-room house but caught herself by remembering she would soon be in the same straits.

"Tova, you rest for a moment. Let me help you."

Tova wiped her brow and sank to sit on the family's sleeping platform. "Thank you, Judith. You must be an angel."

Judith felt a pang of conscience but brushed it away like a spider's web. "I'll need help before long. I think I felt him move today. It was very faint."

"It starts out that way," Tova agreed. "Soon the baby rolls and kicks so hard you know for sure. Ay! Yes, little one. Here, put your hand here," she said, placing her friend's hand on the top of her belly.

Judith felt a series of strong kicks. "I can't wait until my son can do that."

"Unfortunately this little one chooses to move around just as I'm drifting off to sleep at night. No wonder I'm tired. It sounds like you're convinced you're having a boy. Everyone thinks I'm carrying a boy too since I didn't gain much weight except in front. I'm not sure, though."

"I've been asking for a boy," Judith said confidently, careful not to reveal to whom she was praying. "I think it will be. Benjamin would be thrilled. Don't you want a son?"

"Yes, but if Adonai wills, there will be other children. Menachem says if I bear him a daughter, we will simply have to try again. I think it's his way of letting me know either a boy or a girl is fine with him."

After Judith returned home, Tova sat near her hearth and mixed barley flour and water with a little honey to make bread. She was down to the last honey comb, but she craved a bit of sweetness.

Her thoughts turned to Judith's confidence that she would have a son and her friend's visit to their girlhood home. Judith hadn't spoken of her time there except to bring Tova greetings from her family. *What did Judith get caught up in at the festival?*

Tova remembered her first festival when she was thirteen. Their families settled close to Rabbah's walls for a few nights. Late one night Judith had tried to introduce Tova to the "fun" of the festival. She dragged Tova to Moloch's shrine where a group of slightly older boys had congregated. "Have a good time for once, Tova," she said before selecting the most handsome dark-haired boy and disappearing into an alcove off the courtyard.

Tova shrank into the shadows of the wall, but a couple of the boys tried to entice her to accompany them into the courtyard. Tova was relieved when another group of worshippers approached the temple and she could quietly escape.

Three months later, she had been gathering fuel for the fire when she overheard her oldest brother arguing with their serving maid Opal. "It's not mine," her brother affirmed.

"Don't you remember the festival? Of course, my baby's yours," the girl said.

Tova froze behind the rock hiding her from their view.

"I remember. There were lots of girls. I'm sure you had lots of men too."

"No, just you. All I wanted was you."

When the silence stretched so long Tova thought they had walked away, she peeked around the rock. Her brother looked like a cornered ram. "Fine. It's mine, but I'm not taking you as a wife, or a concubine. Sacrifice it to Moloch." He stomped away, leaving Opal with her mouth gaping like a fish's.

Over the next six moons, Tova watched their servant closely. The cheeky girl's steps slowed as her figure blossomed. Tova was surprised her mother didn't dismiss her.

Tova was trying to make lentil soup one afternoon when a primal scream ripped through the air. She froze, uncomprehending. Her mother and sisters had gone to trade with neighbors, and the men were tending the goats. Had a wild dog wandered into their camp? The next scream shrieked her name.

Opal had done little work the last two days, and Tova had forgotten about her. Now she needed help--immediately. Tova had never seen a baby birthed. One of her older sisters had two little ones, but her husband's family had assisted her. Tova loved the dark-eyed babes, but her stomach churned at the thought of helping at a birth.

Slowly, she approached the goatskin tent housing the girl, dreading what she would see. Another strangled cry compelled her to lift the flap and check on the suffering mother. Opal was squatting in a corner. The smell overpowered Tova, but the look of relief on Opal's face caused her to say, "I'll get some water and be right back."

She stumbled out of the tent into the clean, dry air and took deep breaths. Hurrying to a water jug, she hefted it into her arms and returned. Picking up a clean square of cloth from a pile on the sleeping mat, she poured a bit of the precious liquid on the rag and wiped Opal's forehead. This close, she could see the tears and the fear. She grasped a damp hand. Opal gestured toward a smooth stick on the mat, and Tova fetched it. Opal put it in her mouth and bit down hard as her body tensed. Then she took it out and panted, "Thank you. Soon. Catch the baby?"

Tova nodded wordlessly. Two more pushes and a warm, slippery body filled her hands. The girl collapsed backwards in exhaustion as Tova looked in confusion at a cord running from the baby's belly up into its mother. She tugged gently but it seemed attached.

Why couldn't people be more like goats? She'd witnessed plenty of goats give birth. The kids fell to the ground. The dams licked them clean, and soon they stood up and butted around, searching for milk. Unfortunately, this baby and mother weren't going to follow suit.

Eyes closed, the mother was massaging her stomach, and the baby was beginning to mewl. When he started to cry, Opal opened her eyes and held out her arms. Tova had never seen such a look in a woman's eyes, tender and love-filled, all fear and pain wiped away. Amazed, she sat back on her heels as the mother surveyed the tiny, wrinkled newborn. Rousing herself, she dampened another cloth and handed it to Opal, who gently began cleaning her new charge.

"We'll need a knife," Opal whispered.

Tova flinched. *For what?* But Opal seemed to know what to do. Tova ran out to the cook fire. Noticing the soup, she stirred it quickly and moved it to a cooler place, so it wouldn't burn while she was busy.

The baby was attached to his mother's breast when Tova reentered the tent. His head was clean but his back needed attention. "Could you wipe his back?"

Tova rinsed out the cloth, aware of the mother's tremors. Her face radiated love, but she grimaced now and then, as if still experiencing pain.

"I'm sorry to ask, Tova, but I'm not steady enough. Could you cut the cord, right about here?" Opal showed her by clamping her fingers around the cord. Fluid gushed out when Tova complied but stopped as she tied it. She wiped off her hands, but Opal was a mess. Fortunately, the baby had fallen asleep and lost his grip on his mother. Tova finished cleaning him and swaddled him in a wide strip of linen.

She took the slimy afterbirth far away from the camp and buried it. By the time she returned, the soup was burning. Her mother said nothing after ducking in to check on Opal, but there wasn't time to make anything else for dinner.

When her father and brothers tasted the stew, her father roared, crossed the campsite in three strides and struck her across the back. The solid blow knocked her to the sand where she cowered, expecting more. He spared her, probably because of the addition of another male to the family. He usually did a more thorough job. She didn't get anything to eat that night, but it was nothing compared to what would befall Opal and her child.

Opal fashioned a sling to carry her son with her at all times, showering him with attention. In a rare moment when she allowed Tova to watch over him, she said, "Please, keep him with you until I'm back. He's all I have. My family was killed by the Persians."

Tova loved tending her tiny nephew and felt a special bond with him. He was a good baby, rarely crying. Unfortunately, the child's father failed to notice his charms. He ignored Opal and his son as he prepared for marriage into one of Rabbah's merchant families. Tova wished he had kept ignoring them, but when the baby was four moons old, he tied and gagged Opal and took his son to Moloch's shrine. The entire family, except the baby's mother, attended the ceremony.

There was a huge metal statue of the "Lord of darkness." The priests lit a fire in its belly, and Tova's brother put his own son into the idol's metal hands. The flesh sizzled as the babe shrieked. Tova could still hear the innocent's agonized cries over the throb of drums.

Tova determined never to speak to her brother again. Her resolve hardened when she saw him release Opal. The bereft mother wailed and screamed, grasping his robe. He kicked her away. From that day on, she seemed unable to focus on her tasks. When Tova faced her and explained what she should be doing, she saw emptiness in Opal's dark eyes. Tova's brothers and father beat her repeatedly for her absent-mindedness, but the punishments made no difference. One night Opal wandered off into the desert and never returned.

Tova never forgave her brother, and she loathed Moloch. She refused to go to the shrine over the next year, feigning illness. She felt relieved when she was asked to visit Judith in Gibeon.

Then Menachem the Jew offered her family a bride price. Her family accepted eagerly, like they wanted to be rid of her. They didn't even come for the wedding. She didn't miss them, except occasionally her mother. *I've been delivered from a realm of darkness and evil, and I'm never going back. Why does Judith want to?*

Chapter 16

Esther sat on the balcony outside her bedroom in Susa, admiring the garden but too fatigued to stroll in it. She turned her thoughts to Hadassah and offered a prayer for her. *Keep Hadassah and all Ezra's band safe as they travel to Jerusalem and settle there, Adonai. The psalmist wrote, "Weeping may endure for a night but joy comes in the morning." Make this true for my beloved Hadassah.*

Her elderly maid Atossa limped through the doorway from Esther's suite of rooms, "Company, Your Highness."

Esther motioned to signify the newcomer could enter her presence. No one had visited her in days. She smiled when Nehemiah's sturdy frame appeared.

"Shalom, Nehemiah."

"Shalom, Your Highness. I bear a message from the King. He desires your presence in two days' time at a banquet with envoys from Nubia. He asks if you are well and offers the use of a palanquin to bring you to the hall."

Esther considered her deteriorating health. "I can manage if a palanquin is sent."

"The king will rejoice."

"Could you sit with me for a short time?"

"I have no pressing matters to attend and would like nothing better," Nehemiah replied gallantly, settling on a couch. Silence stretched like a web, connecting them on the drowsy late morning. "I have always wanted to hear about your time in the palace."

"I'm sure the palace gossip has twisted the stories."

"They portray you as the heroine you are, but I'd like to hear the stories from your own lips."

Esther reflected on the tragedies in her own life—being ripped from the Jewish community by Persian guards, losing her adopted son Sparamizes to a poisoning, and experiencing Xerxes' end. "I'll speak to you of one of my darkest nights. You'll know I'm no heroine.

"King Xerxes called for me the night he died. When I arrived at his bed chamber, I found him on the floor in a pool of blood. A dagger had been plunged into his chest. He was almost, but not quite…gone. I sat on the floor and held his head in my lap," Esther steadied her voice. "He never opened his eyes or spoke, but I think he sensed I was there. He let out a little sigh when I first touched him and told him to hold on, the court physician was coming. But when the physician arrived, he pronounced my husband dead." Esther stared unseeing at the sun-drenched gardens.

"I felt as though a gaping hole had ripped me open. Even all these years later, I feel the loss of him. He was always good to me, but I saw how he treated his concubines and subjects. It wasn't kind, or even fair. He inspired fear in people. He hung my favorite guard after our son Sparamizes was poisoned. It wasn't Otanes' fault, but Xerxes had to make an example of someone, and he chose my most dedicated guard, simply because he had been on duty." Esther's thoughts turned to her despair at Sparamizes' death and outrage at Otanes' execution.

After a long pause, Nehemiah prompted, "You were talking about the night the king died."

"I couldn't pull myself away from his body, and the guards let me stay. Artabanus, the head bodyguard, had vaulted from a window to pursue the murderer through the palace grounds, and the other guards didn't know what to do except stay in the bed chamber with me and the body.

"Before the moon rose, Artabanus returned with Darius, who was almost too drunk to stand and certainly hadn't stabbed his father. But Artabanus ran him through with a sword, shouting 'Justice for the king!' The men were mutilating Darius, so I crept away as quietly as I could, begging God to spare me and Arty. I recognized the threat to Arty, who had just entered manhood. Only the Most High could shield us now, but He had delivered me before.

"I went to my rooms and sent Atossa for Artaxerxes. Thanks be to God—Artaxerxes reached my room safely with his contingent of guards. We sent the youngest for other men we trusted and amassed as many guards as we could. Fortunately, these tower rooms can be barricaded against an attack. Sheer numbers could successfully breach it, but though I watched all night, I saw only a handful of men pass by. Most were too drunk to pose any threat except to themselves."

"What a shame that Mordecai had retired from his position!"

"Yes, well, my adoptive father was an old man by then, and ruling the kingdom under Xerxes' command could be exhausting... and thankless. The next morning the seven princes of Persia sent for me and Artaxerxes to present ourselves. Surrounded by a score of loyal guards, we approached the *apadana*. Tarshish spoke for the princes, 'Xerxes, most magnificent king of Persia, was wickedly murdered during the second watch. The murderer, first in line to the crown, is dead. Artaxerxes is our new monarch.' My heart had almost slowed to its regular rhythm when he continued, 'Since he is not of age to rule the lands of our empire, Artabanus will act as regent.'

"During that long night, I had figured out who assassinated Xerxes. Darius was too drunk to harm his father. Although he hated his father and would gladly have murdered him, he could barely stand. Once the shock wore off, I realized Artabanus was the assassin. No one else could have gotten in and out of the chamber undetected. And now he had control of the kingdom! But I had no recourse. The princes' decision was final. I should have quit cowering in my room at first light and tried to speak with them, but it was too late."

"My father was present in the apadana. He told me you faced the princes of Media and Persia and regally dipped your head in acquiescence. He said there was profound silence when

74

Tarshish placed the crown on Artaxerxes' head, and every person in the room prostrated himself before the teenaged king."

"I'm glad I didn't look as scared as I felt. Your father was a good man. The palace lost a valuable scribe when he left us for paradise last year."

"Mother and I miss him."

"The way you support your mother is to be commended."

Nehemiah shifted uncomfortably, "On the day we were speaking of, all the scribes' quills, including my father's, scratched furiously across the scrolls, proclaiming the news of Xerxes' murder, Artaxerxes' coronation, and Artabanus' regency to the entire empire."

"I told Arty what I suspected, and we were vigilant. I know I aged a lot in the next few months." Esther fingered her graying hair. "I was terrified for Arty. The one good thing that came out of that time was you, Nehemiah. To prevent poisoning, Artaxerxes was given food and drink testers as soon as he began eating solid food. But as you know, the old man who served as cupbearer had died, and Mordecai found a young Jew to fill his position. I'm thankful for your moderating influence on the king."

"He needs someone to confide in."

"Yes, and you know when to listen and when to offer a solution." Esther sighed. "You saw the rest of the story play out. Artaxerxes trained exceptionally hard with his weapons following his father's murder. You were at the banquet he planned for me, Mordecai, and Artabanus."

"It was exactly three moons after Xerxes' death."

"Yes, but I missed the significance at first. Artaxerxes plied Artabanus with the kingdom's best wines while drinking sparingly. He sent Artabanus' bodyguard on a mission, disarmed Artabanus of his own sword, and pierced his chest, shouting, 'For my father!'"

"His aim was true, and Artabanus died quickly. You realize Artaxerxes wasn't safe as long as Artabanus lived?"

"At first I shook so badly I needed Mordecai to assist me back to my room, but he told me the same thing. I'd never thought of

Arty as so…bloodthirsty, but that night he proved he was a true Persian monarch," Esther finished sadly.

"Our king is strong without being cruel. It had to be done."

"I wish I hadn't been witness to the deed."

"Artaxerxes realized he had upset you. It wasn't his intention. He talked with me about it. He thought you would be pleased to see the justice he exacted for your husband's life. He also wanted to assure you of your safety because of his strength. Neither he nor you were at the mercy of Artabanus anymore."

"The regent had no mercy."

"Exactly. He craved power and would have stopped at nothing to keep it."

"I suppose you're right, but I never wanted more bloodshed."

Chapter 17

I can't take the dust," Naama grumbled as the three friends trudged along. "I miss those days of walking by the Euphrates River and being able to rinse off at night and soak my feet."

"At least you're not sick every morning," Hadassah tried to encourage her.

"And you have good energy," Jarah added.

"True. Some of the women my grandmother treated were tired the entire time they were pregnant. They never would have been able to walk like this. I actually want to hurry, so we can get to Tadmor and sell a small rug my mother sent with me. She said it would get a good price and help us finish the journey."

"What kind of designs does your mother use?" Jarah asked.

"She weaves shapes into most of her rugs. Occasionally a client wants animals like lions or elk. She can make curves but doesn't do them often because they're difficult and those rugs take more than a year to complete. She's done two or three for extremely wealthy buyers."

"The queen had a gorgeous rug the size of a large tent. It was red and blue with wavy lines like a river," Hadassah said.

"It sounds like one of her rugs, but I know she never received a commission from the palace."

"It was from the house of a nobleman named Haman. King Xerxes gave his property to Esther after he executed Haman. She gave it to Mordecai, but he brought her a stunning rug that had been Haman's. Mordecai said it was too fine for his dirt floor but would make a great surface for little Arty to play on."

"Haman was the king's chief advisor right around the time you were born," Jarah added. "He concocted a plan to kill all the Jews in the kingdom and got Xerxes to approve it. Neither of them knew Esther was a Jew. When she pleaded for her people's lives, the king chose to listen to her instead of Haman. You know—it's what our Purim celebration's all about."

"We never talked about Purim much. Sometimes friends sent mother presents, but she never sent any. My em doesn't like to talk about palace doings much, probably because of my father."

"I don't think I've ever heard you mention your father," Jarah said.

"He was a palace guard. He and another guard were the ones who found Esther in Susa and took her to be part of the harem. My mother did tell me he was devoted to the queen. He believed she was an exceptional person. The day he found Esther he told my mother she might become the next queen. He became one of her personal bodyguards after she was crowned, but the king executed him a couple of years later."

"Your father was Otanes?" Hadassah asked.

"Yes."

"I'm sorry, Naama. I remember when that happened. Esther's son Sparamizes was poisoned, and the king blamed your father for not protecting him. The queen didn't fault your dad. She often told me how much she valued your father and how much she missed him. She was crushed when the king ordered his death."

"Not like my mother was. She never recovered," Naama replied bitterly.

"No, of course not. No one mourns a man like his wife," Jarah soothed. Belatedly realizing how her comment might affect Hadassah, she tried to gauge the widow's reaction from the corner of her eye.

The three women kept moving through the parched, barren sand. Even Jarah could think of nothing to cheer them.

Chapter 18

Jarah had never seen Naama as happy as she was following a day's rest in Tadmor.

"Ariel got a great price for my rug, and he spent a coin on oranges for me, saying the baby will benefit. He wouldn't let Gili have one, but I slipped him a section of mine when Ariel went to look after the donkey."

Jarah laughed. "Did you share with your husband too, or just your husband's cousin?"

"I gave Ariel some when Gili was gathering dung for the morning's fire. Now I only have two left, but they won't keep long in this heat. We can enjoy them at the noonday rest. What did you do in the city?"

"We went with Hadassah's sisters to a sulphuric spring to bathe."

"Ick. Just the smell was enough to make me feel sick. Why bathe in it?"

"It's supposed to have healing properties," Hadassah explained. "I think my skin looks a little less rough now. It's taken a beating from the sun and dust these last two moons."

"We needed extra oil to get the stink out of our hair," Jarah added.

"I heard an Arab sheik offered us archers for protection, but your father refused," Naama said. "What about the caravan that was attacked before it reached Damascus?"

"Except for that one incident, it's been peaceful for many moons," Hadassah answered. "And the *protection* cost more than we can afford."

"Oren says the Arabs probably made up the story so they

could get some gold from us. We're not experienced like the caravans of merchants. They wouldn't scare as easily."

"I don't know," Naama said uneasily. "We're carrying plenty of silver and gold. Wouldn't it be worthwhile to give them a little of it, if we could deliver the rest safely?"

"The treasure is for the temple. My father believes the Most High will be our shield and protector."

"I hope he's right."

"Adonai will deliver us from evil," Jarah said confidently.

∞∞∞

"I'm glad we've reached Damascus safely," Naama said as the three friends admired the date palms peeking over the horizon. "I can breathe a bit easier now."

"The Damascenes may have tales to scare us with too," Jarah said.

"We'll see. I can't wait to wash off this grit and spend a day with my feet up."

"Soon we'll be in Jerusalem," Hadassah added wearily.

"Really?" Jarah asked excitedly. "I can't wait to see the temple."

"If all goes well, it should only take three more weeks," Hadassah responded.

"Are you going to live in Jerusalem, Jarah?" Naama asked.

"For a while. Since Oren's family hasn't been fulfilling their Levitical duties for quite some time, we'll stay at least a few moons. We also don't know what's happened to his family's home in Gibeon. We'll need to make a quick trip out there to see."

"Gibeon?" Naama's face lit up. "Ariel and Gili's vineyards are there. This is wonderful. I'll know someone in my town! If I weren't so tired I'd dance to celebrate. Will you help me when the baby comes?"

Jarah laughed. "Absolutely! To think I'll already have a friend in my home town. We should be settled in Gibeon by the time your baby comes. Wild camels won't be able to keep me away!"

The women giggled at that picture.

"I'm sure Ariel could check on Oren's familial home and send word about its condition," Hadassah said sensibly.

"Great idea! I'll tell Oren as soon as I see him."

"That should be soon. The men stopped and are setting up camp," Naama said.

Chapter 19

After a Sabbath's rest in Damascus, the caravan traveled swiftly. Ezra was eager to reach Dan, the northern boundary of Israel's land. Skirting Mt. Hermon between Damascus and Dan, Jarah thrilled to walk in the land of her people. Dan had long been considered the northernmost point in the kingdom, although it wasn't currently inhabited by Jews. When the caravan reached Jerusalem in two weeks, she would finally worship at the temple.

Hadassah was staying close to her sister Adin, who had a slight fever, so Jarah and Naama were on their own as they exclaimed over the cooler temperature near the mountain. "I don't ever want to walk through a desert again!" Naama declared.

Evidently, Naama had become resigned to living out her days in Yehud since there was no way home except back through the desert, but Jarah didn't point that out. Naama had lamented leaving her mother and friends daily for the first half of their trip. Now she only mentioned them occasionally. "I agree with you, sister!"

She didn't realize a long silence had fallen until Naama said tentatively, "I know you and Hadassah think I'm a spoiled child to resist returning to Yehud with my husband."

"You're leaving more behind than either of us, Naama. You're also younger than we are. You reacted differently."

"You're both escaping something in Susa," Naama continued. "My life was there."

Jarah thought about what she had escaped. "You're right. I escaped living as a maiden, unwanted by my uncle. Hadassah

82

escaped life in the harem. You're wiser than we give you credit for."

Naama smiled a little and then sobered. "Do you think you could tell me something, Jarah? Why doesn't Hadassah like me?"

Jarah paused, startled by the depth of Naama's perception.

"You're not the only one who can be blunt."

"I guess not. It's not that Hadassah doesn't like you..."

Naama flipped her hand impatiently.

"No. Let me finish. I'm going to be honest with you."

"I wouldn't expect you to be anything else."

"She aches for what you have, Naama—a husband and child on the way. And sometimes, especially when we first met you and you were miserably sick, you didn't seem to value either."

"I see. I was afraid it was me. She's been kind to me, of course, but sometimes I sensed. . . something else. Do you think she'll remarry? Gili would like to find a wife."

"I think he's a bit young for her," Jarah said gently.

"You mean immature, don't you? Yes, you're right. We'll have to look for someone else, but most of the men in the caravan are married or too young."

"I think Adonai will bring along the right man when she's ready."

"It wouldn't hurt for us to keep our eyes open."

The Bactrians waited in taut anticipation. Ctesias had ordered them to kill the men, but they could do with the women and children as they wished. He was sure many would become spoils of the battle. He could use a woman himself. He would pick the most beautiful one before the men made their choices.

Ctesias had positioned his forty-nine men in the crags of the Upper Galil. They had passed Ezra's band when the Jews rested in Damascus on their holy day. They would regret that pause now, he thought gleefully. He would pin them between his men and the swamps to the east, his archers raining down arrows on their unsuspecting heads.

Hazor lay half a parasang to the south. The townspeople would hear nothing. His mercenaries had provisioned there last night and then camped in these hills to familiarize themselves with the terrain. Now they crouched behind brush and boulders as their prey advanced into sight. "Aim for the man on the light-colored donkey," he instructed his best archer, positioned nearby.

As the vanguard of the caravan drew into range, a noise from the direction of Hazor distracted the attackers. Craning their necks toward the commotion, Ctesias and his men lowered their weapons in disbelief. A welcoming party of villagers was spilling down the road. At its head strode the chieftain who had greeted the Bactrians yesterday.

"Curse their hospitality!" Ctesias muttered. He made a few swift hand motions to indicate his soldiers should hold their positions.

As the headman and Ezra shouted introductions, Ctesias' lieutenant whispered, "Can't we take out all of them?"

"No. We would have surprised and scattered Ezra's people, but some of them would have reunited and continued. We can't risk attacking people who can identify us, since at least a few of them would escape too. They know this land much better than we do. Foiled again!" Ctesias felt like screaming but hunkered down for an extended wait while the travelers and their hosts greeted each other and headed into town.

As the refreshed travelers passed south of Hazor and through Beth Shan, they admired the lush land. Although the grain had been harvested months before, the vineyards were bursting with grapes. The fig and pomegranate trees provided succulent fruit for a welcome addition to their regular diet of bread and dried fruit.

"Have you ever seen such grapes, Ariel?" Gili laughed. "We'll be able to make the best wine east of the Great Sea with these."

"We haven't reached our land yet, Gili. I think they get more rain here. We'll have to see."

Naama saw her husband's worried brow. *If his family's vines produce this well, someone had surely claimed them. How will we get the land back? And where will we live if we can't?*

I wish we stayed in Susa. Naama sighed. *How are you, em? Are you well? You're going to have another grandchild, but you won't know about him until after the birth. I'll get word to you somehow.*

The residents of Shechem failed to greet the returnees. They stared as Ezra's group drew water from the town's well, but said little. "Why do they dislike us?" Hadassah asked her father.

"They're Samaritans. Zerubbabel didn't allow them to help rebuild the temple. They worship both their gods and the Most High on that mountain," he said, pointing to Mt. Gerizim. "It's ironic really. Did you notice the huge stone next to the ancient oaks before the well?"

"Yes, it looked like it had been placed there."

"It was. By Joshua. He had it placed there after our people conquered the Canaanites and promised to serve Elohim alone and not idols. And look at all that's happened since—carried away by the Assyrians and Babylonians for failure to keep our word. Now a few of us return—to a land inhabited by idol worshippers."

"It would have been good to buy fruit from them."

"They wouldn't have given you a fair price, daughter. Don't fret. We're on the ridge road to Jerusalem. In just two days, we will finally be *home*."

Home. Where is home? I spent most of my life in a Persian palace, but home was Jedidiah. Will I ever feel at home again?

Chapter 20

The next day the travelers reached Ramah. Several small groups had already split off from the main party as they traveled the ridge road from Shechem. Those returnees were anxious to see their ancestral homes but swore to Ezra they would journey to Jerusalem for Yom Kippur.

Today Naama's family would leave the caravan for the short walk across the plain to Gibeon. She embraced Jarah and Hadassah. "We'll send word about your husband's property as soon as possible."

"We should be coming back to Gibeon before your baby arrives. Five moons, little one," Jarah said to her belly. "No early arrivals."

"When you visit the temple, look for me," Hadassah added. "Ask any of the priests or Levites. They'll know where my father's chambers are."

"I don't know when I'll be up to making the trip," Naama answered.

"Won't you be coming for Yom Kippur?"

All Jews were expected to worship in Jerusalem for Passover, the Feast of Tabernacles, and Yom Kippur. Ezra had taught them these requirements when he read the laws to them every Sabbath. "I won't be in any shape to travel in three moons," she said, looking at her mounded stomach.

Who will care for me? Ariel and Gili committed to go to the Temple for the Day of Atonement. I don't relish staying by myself in a strange place, but by then I might feel more settled. Surely not all of the women will travel to Jerusalem. Some might be in my condition or have children too young to go.

"Probably not," Jarah agreed.

"If your baby's a boy, you'll come to dedicate him, won't you?" Hadassah asked.

Naama didn't know anything about dedicating sons, but agreement seemed the expected response. "Yes."

"Good. And if she's a girl, I hope to meet her before she's weaned."

"I'm sure I can make such a short trip before this child's weaned." Naama became serious. "Thank you both for helping me through this journey. I don't know how I would have managed without the two of you."

Jarah smiled. "The Almighty had it all planned." She hugged Naama again. "Take care," she whispered.

Chapter 21

Tova and Judith watched curiously as a dusty group of about two dozen travelers spoke with the elders at Gibeon's city gate. Tova sat back from their task of grinding and rested her hands on her ample belly. The baby would arrive in about a moon's time. Judith continued pounding the barley with a mortar, but slowed to look frequently at the newcomers. Before she finished grinding, one of the elders ushered a large part of the group into the city and toward the dilapidated limestone huts at the far end. Many houses lay in ruins since Gibeon's population had never recovered from the exile. A younger man led a half score behind the city walls.

"Tova, I think they're moving here."

"You must be right. Otherwise the elders would be finding families with room to put them up for the night."

"They can't sleep in those hovels. The roofs are scattered over the floors."

"Not in every house. A few of them are solid. I don't think there will be enough houses for all the families though. Where do you think the ones led outside the city are going? One of those women looked pregnant!" Tova resumed grinding.

"Maybe they have relatives outside the city."

"They're going to need supplies. If we work fast, we'll have extra grain to give them. It's too late to make bread today, but they can bake it tomorrow. I saw a few children. Could you milk our goat for me? I can't do it anymore. Menachem usually takes care of it when he comes in for supper, but this way we could take it over with the grain, and they can have it for their evening meal."

"I'll help you grind a little longer. It won't take me long to milk."

"Good. There's a skin for the milk behind the door."

∞∞∞∞

Ariel, Gili, and Naama surveyed their familial land from a slight rise. Naama cuddled the kid goat Hadassah had given her at parting. Hadassah's goats had produced several offspring on the journey, and she had given Naama one. Drinking its milk would help her unborn child grow strong. Hadassah had been a good friend on the journey, although she had never shown Naama the warmth she shared with Jarah. *Will Hadassah and I continue to be friends in this new land where we'll rarely see each other? At least Jarah will settle here soon so I'll have one friend.*

Naama sighed as she inspected their bleak allotment. The vines to their right were scraggly, but she could see bunches of grapes on them if she squinted. In a smaller plot to the left, she was encouraged to see more greenery. The leaves hid any fruit hanging on those vines. A well-appointed, obviously inhabited limestone house nestled at the side of the hill, but no one was in sight.

Ariel avoided the right section, and the trio ventured into the rows on the left. As they neared the far end of the vineyard, they found a small white house. The walls appeared solid, but the roof had caved in. Naama sneaked a look at her husband, trying to judge his reaction. He would speak carefully for her sake, but his face would reveal his gut reaction.

"Someone has been caring for the vines close to the other house and will claim the fruit," Gili said. "But no one has pruned these vines for years."

"But look over here," Ariel added as they walked along a terrace toward the derelict house. "No one's living in this house, so we'll have shelter." He turned to his wife. "Don't worry. We have the tent until Gili and I can fix the roof. It shouldn't take more than a week." He looked at the debris on the dirt floor. "We'll haul all this out and find branches to lay across the top. Mixed with plaster, the roof will keep the rain out."

Naama hoped he didn't expect her to help as she hadn't the slightest idea how to make plaster.

Ariel continued, "I'll find someone to show us how to make plaster from what's available. It shouldn't be too hard."

Gili had already disappeared into the leafy vines past the house. "The fruit's sparse this year, but we can improve the crop for next year. And we can probably have the little growing this year if we harvest it. It certainly doesn't look like anyone's laid claim to it." The three gazed soberly at the small vineyard.

"Do you think two families can live off it?" Naama asked a little anxiously.

"We'll manage," Ariel answered reassuringly.

"When we present our claim to our fathers' land at the city gate, the other vineyard will be restored to us too," Gili said.

Naama noted the grim set of her husband's mouth. He wasn't convinced by Gili's words.

"Let's pitch the tent for Naama and start carrying the debris out of the house. We can eat late," Ariel said, beginning to unpack the donkey he was leading.

Naama set down her goat and began unpacking pottery and foodstuffs so she could prepare bread. It would be unleavened tonight, but tomorrow she would have all day to make proper loaves because, finally, they were home.

Tova happily reported the news she had gleaned when she and Judith took their contributions to the new families. "Menachem, they're crowded into the three houses with the best roofs. One has a small hole, but I don't think it will rain tonight."

"As many men as can be spared from the vineyards will help them make repairs tomorrow. We should be able to finish a few more. Did they have enough provisions for the evening meal?"

"I think so. All our neighbors took some type of food to them. We took ground barley, pomegranates, and a skin of milk."

"You should be drinking the milk right now, for the baby."

"I didn't think missing it one day would hurt. I gave it to a family with two skinny children. The journey from Babylon must have been difficult."

"Benjamin heard they came with about two thousand people led by a priest named Ezra. Most continued on to Jerusalem, but about five hundred have broken off from the main group to return to the villages of their forefathers."

"It's a good thing only a few came here. Even with the good barley harvest, I don't know how we'd feed many more mouths."

"Adonai will provide. We'll get by until next year when there will be more hands to plant a bigger crop. It *is* good to have more Jews living here in Gibeon. It makes the city more secure from marauders."

More of Ezra's group was likely to settle in Gibeon after they transacted their business in Jerusalem. Menachem hoped that by the time Tova heard of it or saw them come through the city gates, she would see the positive side of their arrival. He wanted her to stay as calm as possible until the baby arrived.

Chapter 22

Entering Jerusalem and following its ancient streets to the temple absorbed Jarah's attention, but the tumbled stones and gates concerned Oren. "It looks like this place was attacked recently, not more than a hundred years ago," he said in consternation. "What a disgrace!"

Jarah's gaze flickered toward the ruins but was caught by the edifices behind them. "Look at the houses. They're impressive."

Oren agreed. "Yes, but with nothing protecting them, they might not stay that way. If the city had walls, it could hold out against enemies while the satrap sent help. Since there is no wall, raiders could ransack the city and melt into the wilderness before soldiers could catch them."

Jarah's eager smile started to fade. Trying to lessen the impact of his words, Oren said, "Gibeon should be safer since it's walled."

"But the temple could be pillaged again."

"Why would the Most High raise up Zerubbabel to rebuild and then allow it to be destroyed right away? We know he allowed the Babylonians to destroy it because of our idolatry. We won't make that mistake again, and Ezra's coming back to make sure *all* the people know God's laws, not just the priests. I'm sure the temple will be fine."

"Our enemies might not destroy it, but they could take all this gold and silver we're bringing back."

"It's a miracle this treasure came back from Babylon in the first place. It belongs to the Most High. He'll take care of it *and* His house."

"Maybe we could work on rebuilding the wall." Jarah lifted

her face to consider how high the wall would be and to catch the cooling afternoon breeze.

Oren threw back his head and laughed. "I don't think you and I could do such a big job by ourselves, especially since you're eager to get back to your friend in Gibeon. We'll see what Ezra plans once he sees the condition of the city."

Jarah smiled at the picture of the two of them piling rock to refortify Jerusalem. Some strong sons would speed rebuilding. But at this point they didn't even have an infant son, or the signs of one coming.

Oren interrupted her musings. "Let's go to the temple right away. Do you remember the words of all the psalms Ezra taught us?"

"I think so. Which one did Ezra say was sung as pilgrims approached the temple?"

"I was glad when they said to me, 'Let us go to the house of the LORD,'" Oren began to sing in a wobbly tenor.

Jarah took up the words in her clear soprano, and soon the returnees around them were singing too, drawing the inhabitants of Jerusalem into their train to see the newcomers' reactions to the temple.

Jarah's voice soared on the words, "Pray for the peace of Jerusalem, 'May they prosper who love you. May peace be within your walls...'" She started praying fervently that there would *be* walls—protective, solid walls. Soon.

Hadassah sang the psalms in a soft harmony drowned by Rebekah's lusty soprano. The Jewish entourage swept through a wide gate in a woven wood fence, paused for the ceremonial washings, and entered the temple's outer courtyard. The women moved to the perimeter as Ezra and the men ascended into the inner courtyard to greet the high priest and his attendants. Over a thousand Jews crowded into the courtyards and others spilled over into the street.

Hadassah caught sight of Jarah on the other side. Jarah's plain face was lit with an ethereal light as she sang, radiating love for Adonai and awe at standing in his house. *"The Lord has done great things for us, and we are filled with joy,"* Hadassah thought. The phrase echoed in her mind and stayed with her for the rest of the celebration.

∞∞∞∞

After the day's activities, Ezra had difficulty falling asleep in his chamber near the temple, so he rose and lit an oil lamp. He was glad for the solitude after weeks of traveling with hundreds of people. He could finally think in peace, rather than answer endless questions.

When the family ate, he had noticed Hadassah's excitement about the temple. It had been months since she'd shown enthusiasm about anything. Tonight her glowing face reminded him of the joy on her wedding day when he spoke the words joining her to Jedidiah. Such a fine man. *May she find a new life here with a good husband, Lord, and bless them with a quiver full of children.*

"The Lord has done great things for us, and we are filled with joy" were the words Hadassah had shared as they ate the evening meal. *She's right. Three hundred parasangs with all the precious vessels for the Temple, and never a skirmish with bandits! The fact that King Artaxerxes commissioned us to return in the first place. Now the opportunity to teach the people Adonai's laws and establish bet 'amma's. The people will honor Torah, and we'll be able to stay in the land promised to us.*

With a full heart, Ezra began to write: "When the Lord brought back the captives to Zion, we were like men who dreamed. Our mouths were filled with laughter, our tongues with songs of joy. Then it was said among the nations, 'The Lord has done great things for them.'" He added Hadassah's words. "The Lord has done great things for us, and we are filled with joy." I'll give the words to one of the Levite singers. They can sing it when we return the vessels to God's house and offer a thank offering for our safe journey.

Chapter 23

Even from a distance, Tova read the outrage in Judith's gestures and heavy tread. Mopping her brow, she settled back and braced herself for the onslaught.

"The nerve of them! The nerve! Some of those vagabonds who came into the city yesterday moved into the far end of *our* vineyard. And that's not all—they're claiming the whole vineyard's theirs. My dowry! Because their ancestors lived there five generations ago! Who do they think they are?"

Tova was speechless. *Why would these people try to take occupied land?*

"They pitched a tent near the deserted house at the back of our property. Benjamin went to talk to them, and they said they're going to petition the elders to restore their ancestors' vineyard. Benjamin tried to explain the property's been in my family for four generations, but they didn't care."

"But why do they think the elders will give your property to them?"

"Benjamin says when Joshua divided the land among the Jews, each family's portion was to remain in the family *forever*. Have you ever heard of such a thing? Jewish law is crazy. The Ammonites would never put up with such reasoning."

"Come, Judith, sit down. I'll get you some cool water. You don't want to overexcite yourself."

"Because of the baby. Yes, but this baby may be homeless!" Judith began to cry. "The land is mine, mine! You know if Benjamin were ever to divorce me, it would return to me so I could support myself. His father told my parents about that Jewish law before we were betrothed."

"Hush, Judith. Benjamin would never divorce you. I've seen the way he looks at you. You take excellent care of him." Tova gestured toward the burnt pot she'd been scrubbing, "Unlike me, you never burn his food."

Judith sniffed the air. "Oh, Tova. How many times do I have to tell you to watch the lentils carefully when they're close to being done? What distracted you this time?"

Glad to divert her friend's attention, Tova said, "I ran out of water, and the lentils weren't *that* close to being done. I went to the spring to draw water, but it takes me longer to walk up and down the steps. I could smell dinner before I walked in the door."

"Doesn't Menachem get angry?"

"Rarely. I was crying about it, but he hugged me and said not to upset myself. He understands the baby slows me down."

"He's a prince, Tova. My brothers beat their wives if the food is burnt. My mother trained me to tend it very carefully. I never saw her burn food, but I suppose my father might have struck her if she had."

"My father didn't react well to burnt food," Tova said, remembering several beatings. Pushing the memories away, she added, "But the sons of Israel don't seem to deal with their wives the same way. It's a good thing I ended up here."

Judith started to laugh, a bit hysterically. "Oh, Tova. What would I do without you?"

Chapter 24

At sunrise, Ezra met with Eliashib, the high priest. Gray-bearded and dignified, the priest welcomed Ezra into his small chamber and settled on a stool, offering Ezra a similar seat. He introduced his sons Joiada, David, and Eli. Several other priests joined them.

Ezra showed them King Artaxerxes' decree. David read it aloud in a rich bass voice. They gasped at the mention of the silver and gold sent with Ezra. They nodded in agreement when David read that no priest or Levite could be taxed and sobered at the injunction for Ezra to appoint judges to punish lawbreakers.

"What did the king send to enrich the God of heaven's temple?" Joiada asked after a short silence.

"All together our people, the king and the Persians sent 100 talents of gold, 650 of silver, 20 gold bowls, two bronze lavers, and many silver cups and bowls. If you will appoint two trustworthy priests, I will have Sherebiah and Hashabiah weigh out the gifts in your presence," Ezra answered.

"We know your trip was long and difficult. Allow your people to rest, and we will weigh out the gold and silver as you have said the day after tomorrow," Eliashib answered.

"Excellent. The gifts are in two of the temple chambers. Could you provide men to double the guard and relieve the returnees? My people want to settle in as quickly as possible."

"How many men do you need?"

"Half a score should suffice since the temple guards are already patroling the temple perimeter."

"Eli, make sure the guards are told to be extra vigilant," Eliashib ordered.

"Of course, Father."

"Could we offer sacrifices as soon as the gifts are presented?" Ezra asked.

"Absolutely. David will help you acquire whatever animals are necessary. You should probably decide on the offerings this morning, so enough rams, lambs, goats and bulls can be purchased."

"Joaida, as soon as Shabbat is over, send messengers to alert our people to the coming sacrifice. Have I forgotten anything?"

"Who should be appointed to receive the gold and silver?" Eli asked.

The priest stroked his beard as he considered. "Meremoth. Go speak with him after you speak to the guards, Eli. We'll weigh the treasure right after the morning sacrifice."

"I could help, Father," Joiada offered.

"In two days' time, won't you be offering the morning sacrifice?"

"Yes," Joiada said, reddening. "I'm sure David or Eli would stand in for me."

"A priest's most important task is performing the sacrifices."

"Of course, Father."

"Eli, I'm sure you can think of another capable priest on your way to speak with Meremoth. Appoint him, and choose two Levites and scribes to record the items as they are weighed. Is there anything else, Ezra?"

"Could you introduce me to one of the Levites skilled in music?"

"Yes. Joiada, please accompany him to the chamber where the sons of Korah practice their music."

As the men scattered to their tasks, Eliashib called to Ezra, "Would you like to help me offer the morning sacrifice in one hour?"

"There's nothing I would rather do."

On their way to the choir's chamber, Joiada didn't speak to Ezra or ask his reason for wishing to meet the singing Levites.

Ezra felt animosity radiating from the younger man but quickly forgot about him after being introduced to a talented Levite named Nathan.

As Ezra hummed the tune he had composed, Nathan strummed his harp and skillfully expanded it. He beckoned a man with a tambourine to join them, then a trumpeter. As the three wove threads of harmony and melody together, Ezra smiled. The song was joyful and majestic, perfect for the occasion.

Chapter 25

J arah wished she could stand with Oren while the burning sacrifice was offered, but the women stood in their own area. Since it was the Sabbath, Ezra and the high priest laid their hands on the heads of two lambs while quickly slaughtering them with knives. On other days of the week, only one lamb would be offered.

The high priest took the blood and sprinkled it on a huge stone altar. Ezra and another priest chopped the lambs into pieces and rinsed the legs and innards before carrying them to the fire and offering them before the Lord.

Jarah wished she had an offering to thank Adonai for all he had done for her, but they owned only their donkey and two goats. She would ask Oren to set up a loom as soon as possible so she could begin weaving. Perhaps when she sold the cloth, Oren would allow her to buy a dove or pigeon for a sacrifice, or maybe he knew how to snare a bird for an offering. He would be at the temple all day, but she would ask him at the evening meal.

Thinking of the evening meal, she worried about what they would eat. She couldn't bake bread on the Sabbath, and there was none left from their journey. She had a few pomegranates and figs. It would be impossible to buy any food today. Hopefully her husband would eat with the priests and not return to their chamber hungry.

Hadassah caught up with her as they left the court of the women after the sacrifice. "Did you see how shabby the high priest's robe is?"

"Yes," Jarah admitted, wishing she hadn't seen its poor condition but picturing the frayed hem. "I always notice cloth. His robe is worn out."

"His robe is supposed to be blue with elaborate embroidery and gold bells around the hem."

"Why do you say that?"

"It's written in the law of Moses."

"Do you know exactly what it should look like?"

"I could ask Father. It's in one of his scrolls, where Moses is instructed how to make the tabernacle."

"God told Moses how to design the high priest's clothes?"

"Yes, and the other priests' also."

Jarah considered Hadassah's words as the pair walked to her room. "Adonai loves beauty."

"I guess so," Hadassah answered. "His plans for the tabernacle sound lovely. Father said the temple is built along many of the same lines, but it's permanent, not a tent like the tabernacle. Since you're a weaver, Father wants you to fashion new robes for the priests. You'll be paid in coin." She paused. "It's a shame the robes can't be ready for the presentation and offerings in two days. Father says the gifts for the temple didn't include cloth."

Jarah's face lit up. "My aunt sent some of the cloth we made together. She wanted to give something for the temple. There's scarlet and blue linen."

"Perfect! How many robes can you make out of what she sent?"

"Only one out of the blue," Jarah said, remembering her aunt's words about the material being for her, but excited to have something she could offer. "Probably two out of the red, if we cut carefully."

"I think we need purple cloth too. I have a veil we can cut up and use on the hem. It used to be the queen's."

"Good. It would be hard to get purple."

"Since we can only make three robes, who should we make them for?" Hadassah asked, a bit anxiously.

"The high priest, definitely, and probably his son, and your father. We can't have them done for the presentation, but we might be able to surprise everyone for next Sabbath. Can you get your sisters to help us?"

"Adin's handy with a needle and thread. I'm sure she'll help."

"Can you go get her and bring one of your father's robes so we can get the proper size?"

"Yes, but how will we know the right length for Eliashib and his son?"

The women considered the problem. "Ask their wives, but swear them to secrecy," Jarah finally said.

"Jarah, theres's one more problem!"

"What?"

"It's the Sabbath today. We can't work until after sunset. And the offerings may take one whole day."

"We can prepare everything we need and plan how to cut the linen. Would Miriam help us this week?"

"I'm sure she can put aside wedding plans for a day or two when she knows how rushed we are. Plus she'll like surprising abba."

It didn't take long to gather their materials and plan three robes. Hadassah read to Jarah and her sisters from one of the Torah scrolls about the priests' clothing so they could make the new robes like the originals. When the sisters retired to their rooms, they promised to return at the morning's first light.

Jarah's thoughts returned to her food dilemma. She set out fruit and lit candles as soon as the sun set, bringing the Sabbath to a close, their first in Jerusalem. She built up a fire and waited for her husband's return.

She was fussing with the sleeping mats and blanket when she heard the door open. The mouth-watering aroma of lamb made her stomach rumble as she turned to greet her husband, eyes fastened on the haunch of meat.

Oren laughed. "This is the portion that is ours for the day. You should see how big your eyes are, Jarah."

"Blessed be Adonai, who knew I had little to set before you tonight!" Jarah bowed her head, and when she raised it again, dampness clung to her lashes. "He is good."

Oren motioned toward the skimpy dinner set out near the

fire. "Have you eaten since the grain we had this morning?"

"No. But say the blessing, husband. Adonai has given us a feast."

"There will be meat every day I work in the temple."

Jarah's eyes widened even more.

"That's how Adonai provides for the priests."

Jarah drew up a stool, Oren set down the crock filled with meat, and they raised their hands in thanksgiving to Adonai.

Chapter 26

B
ut it's our family property," Gili argued.

"So you say," replied the oldest of the village elders.

"We've repeated the lineage for you twice, and our recital agrees with the memories of the blind woman," Ariel pointed out. Whenever Gibeon's elders considered questions of ownership and inheritance, they called the oldest member of the village, blind Avital. She had learned the ancient records from her grandmother and was in turn teaching them to her granddaughter, also named Avital.

"Correct, but you could have learned the genealogy anywhere. It doesn't prove you are who you say."

Another elder in his prime said, "An Ammonite family has owned the vineyard since the Babylonians took your family into captivity. A few years ago, after their last tenant died, one of their daughters married a fine Israelite. The vineyard is her dowry. Her husband Benjamin been cultivating most of it, and now that it's finally producing, you want us to give it to you? This year's harvest is good because of his sweat and toil."

"He'll need laborers for this harvest. We'll urge him to hire you. You have experience, no?" a more conciliatory elder added.

"Yes," Gili said without hesitation. Ariel didn't think the few vines they helped their grandfather tend counted for much experience, but he didn't contradict the younger man. If they observed how the others harvested and pressed the grapes, they should appear competent, and they could learn valuable skills to cultivate their own vines.

"We'll speak to him today. We'll also inquire about the untended vines. You may be able to take possession of them. Meet us here tomorrow in the middle of the first watch when it will be cooler."

$$\infty \infty \infty$$

When the men returned the following evening, Benjamin was sitting on one of the wooden benches with the elders. He was a powerful young man around Ariel's age and wore a slightly worried expression.

"Come, sit," the peacemaking elder said. "We understand you've already met." The men nodded at each other.

"The grapes should be ready next week, and I have need of extra workers. I would be glad to hire you," Benjamin said, with a slightly strained voice. "I can pay one man's wages in wine, as I do the other laborers, and the other's in grapes so you can start with your own winemaking."

"Benjamin has also agreed that you may take possession of the house you're camped near at the far end of the vineyard. We need more time to deliberate about the untended vines. He planned to cultivate the vines as his family expanded. After the harvest, we will settle this matter."

Ariel could feel Gili tense beside him and laid a restraining hand on his arm. "We appreciate the offer of work for this season and gladly accept."

"It's our land!" Gili exploded as soon as they walked out of sight of the village gate.

"What else can we do, Gili? We can't prove to them that we're the descendants of the first landowners. At least we'll have a roof over our heads. Not an important point for the two of us right now, but it's absolutely necessary for Naama and my child. And it will be more comfortable when the rains start in a few moons." He sighed. "I don't like this either, but it's better than nothing."

Gili angrily shook his head and stalked up the rocky path.

Chapter 27

J arah left their chamber with Oren as the sun rose. Today the returned exiles would offer burnt offerings and sin offerings to the Most High. The animals would be completely burnt, so the people wouldn't feast, but many Jews had come into Jerusalem for the ceremony. The rumor of the temple treasure lured many. Jarah wanted to see those riches too. Her uncle's house contained several silver dishes, and her aunt wore gold jewelry, but she had never seen a talent of gold. According to Oren, there were one hundred talents of gold, a fortune none of them had ever seen.

In spite of her curiosity about the gold, mostly she wanted to worship. Oren had snared a pair of plump doves for them to offer after the main sacrifice. They could eat some of the meat for their dinner.

Jarah was barred from the men's court where the precious metals would be weighed in the high priest's presence. She watched as a procession of twelve men led by Sherebiah and Hashabiah solemnly entered the women's courtyard through the double gate. Each of the leaders carried a huge gold basin filled with gold coins. Their adult sons followed with large sacks of gold or baskets of silver coins. Younger boys carried smaller gold basins and silver cups and bowls. Four men lugged two bronze basins that gleamed in the morning sunlight.

Jarah almost chuckled to see them. She had witnessed the exuberance of the boys after a day of caravan travel. Their parents were training them well as temple workers. A pang clutched her heart. She would ask the Almighty for her own son when they offered their sacrifice.

Ctesias stared when he saw fourscore priests laden with riches. Soon it would be his! It would be suicide to overrun the Jews during the day, but his men were scattered throughout the crowd looking for weaknesses in the temple's structure. They would attack at night, killing as many Jews as they could in the process.

Ctesias strode up to the woven wall of sticks to get a closer look. He was shocked when a spear barred the opening into the courtyard full of women. A short, brawny Jew said, "Only the sons and daughters of Abraham can enter this temple."

Ctesias considered thrusting the weapon to one side and pushing his way in when he noticed the curious faces of women and children turning his way. Two more guards were heading to the gate. They were the only grown men in the entire area. Ctesias would stick out like a ram in a flock of ewes if he did gain entrance. Hoping his men were having more success, he mumbled an apology and retreated down the road.

Jarah turned her attention back to the altar after the disturbance at the gate. She imagined the pagan wanted a look at the temple gold. He was dressed like a Persian in his long sleeved coat with a short sword at the hip. He wouldn't understand that a relationship with the Most High was the true treasure available at the temple.

A string of animals waited at the foot of a large stone altar. Eliashib, his sons, and eight other priests stepped forward to sacrifice twelve bulls while Oren and other Levites positioned the new silver bowls below the animals' throats. They caught the blood and handed the vessels to the priests to sprinkle around the altar. Younger priests cut up the bulls and carefully laid them on the altar's grate. Flames licked up the sacrifices as the aroma of cooking meat overcame the stench of blood.

The priests slaughtered rams next. Jarah lost count after a score. When the sun reached its zenith, the younger priests sacrificed countless lambs. As the day reached its warmest hour, twelve goats were brought into the Temple. By this time, the men looked sweaty and tired. All were blood-stained. A few inexperienced priests who had returned with the exiles and had been observing were pressed into service.

One young priest had downy fuzz instead of the beard all Jewish men wore. He killed his goat with only two strokes, faring better than the priest next to him whose goat escaped after his first attempt. Oren and another Levite quickly caught it and returned it to the embarrassed priest. Oren made a cutting motion with his hand along the goat's neck and held the animal while the fellow finished the job. Then he gave subtle directions about how to divide the meat. Suppressing a laugh, Jarah studied the paving stones at her feet, trying to preserve the solemnity of the occasion.

∞∞∞

Joiada, Eli, and David clustered near the tables of showbread. It was late, and most of the priests and Levites had retired.

"What do you think he wants?" Eli asked.

"Seraiah is his great grandfather. He wants to succeed Father as high priest," Joiada answered.

"How did you find that out? The records are incomplete," David said.

"The scribes have been updating them with all the returnees' names, as well as many names of those still in exile."

"But you've been training to be high priest for years!" Eli said.

"I'm not going to step aside," Joiada vowed.

"Has Ezra told anyone he wants to be high priest?" David asked.

"No, he'd be a fool to announce something like that, but he's making key decisions," Joiada said.

"Isn't he consulting with and deferring to Father?" David said.

"We-ll, yes, but he's wise enough to know he can't take over right away. He has a plan. He wants to set up gathering places in each town where Jews can worship and be taught Torah and the prophets."

"But the temple is where we ought to worship!" Eli said.

"Exactly," Joiada answered.

"Not every Jew can travel to Jerusalem for the Sabbath. We've gotten ourselves into all kinds of trouble because the people don't know Torah. I think teaching in the towns would help our people," David said.

"How would we keep track of all the teachers? How could we know they're interpreting Torah properly?" Eli pointed out.

"I'm sure Ezra would train them. Have you listened to him explain Moses? He's a gifted teacher." Joiada and Eli glared at David.

"Whose side are you on?" Eli demanded.

"I don't think Ezra aspires to be high priest. He's already been appointed governor by the king," David insisted. "He's not hungry for power if he wants to give authority to local teachers."

Joiada considered David's words. "Maybe. But keep your ears open, and let me know what you hear."

"Aren't you included in all the meetings between Ezra and Father? You're the one who gets all the information."

"I am, but Ezra might be meeting with other priests."

David shook his head in disgust. "Remember, we did petition Adonai for help around here. You're not acting very grateful for his provision."

Chapter 28

N o sooner had Oren departed for his daily task of fashioning hooks and other implements for the temple than Hadassah, Miriam and Adin appeared at Jarah's door. They had already cut new robes out of the blue and scarlet, using the old robes of Ezra, Eliashib, and Joiada as guides.

According to the scroll Hadassah had read, the high priest's blue robe would need elaborate collar and hem work. Jarah planned to finish only the basic robe for Sabbath. "Can you do the woven work around the collar next week, Hadassah?"

"Yes, I used to sew with the queen. It's one of my few accomplishments."

Jarah stared at her, "I've never met a more accomplished woman than you, Hadassah."

"She never learned to cook," Adin explained. "She thinks she's missing a necessary skill."

"We're teaching her," Miriam said. "She makes good bread."

"We can't live on bread after you marry," Hadassah reminded her sister.

"Adin knows how to cook lentils and stews. And abba brings home meat that's already roasted."

"A woman should still know how to cook," Hadassah insisted. "The queen and I never thought about it. Jedidiah and I ate all our meals at the palace, and for Passover and Sabbath we always joined you."

"You're intelligent, so it won't be hard to learn. You're one of the few women I know who can read Torah scrolls," Jarah said.

"I had a lot of time to practice while I served the queen. I was more of a companion than a servant. She liked to hear me read aloud."

"Do you miss your old life?"

"Some days, like when I burnt the stew this week and wished I didn't have to cook." Hadassah smiled, then sobered. "I do miss Queen Esther. I'll be doing something during the day and suddenly wonder what she's doing, so I'll try to figure it out from the schedule we used to keep. She said she'd write when there's a delegation from the king or a caravan coming to Jerusalem. I should hear from her soon."

Miriam and Adin sewed the seams of Joiada's new garment as they sat on stools facing each other. Hadassah did the more difficult work on the sleeves of her father's robe, and Jarah stitched the high priest's sleeves with a bone needle.

Before the sun reached its zenith, Miriam said, "I'm not done with the plain stitching on this collar, but I need to grind barley for tomorrow's bread. Do you want me to take your grain too, Jarah? Then you can keep sewing."

Reluctant to burden Miriam with her work, Jarah hesitated. Miriam grabbed the basket of grain from the hearth. "I'd rather grind than sew any day."

"Thank you, Miriam."

"Adin, I forgot to bring the purple veil we're going to cut up and use on the high priest's hem," Hadassah added. "Why don't you go back with Miriam, have a bite to eat, and bring the veil back with you? Don't hurry. Get a breath of air and some sunshine."

When the two sisters left, Jarah offered Hadassah a handful of figs and dates and a dipperful of water. The two seamstresses ate quickly and resumed work. Jarah was beginning to wonder about Adin when the door flew open. Although the light would have helped with their sewing, they had decided to keep the wooden door closed to maintain the secrecy of their project. Now the sunlight blinded her, but she could make out a man's shape. He was gripping a struggling teen.

She didn't realize it was Adin until Hadassah shouted, "How dare you touch my sister!" When the man released the child,

Hadassah caught the weeping girl and sheltered her in her arms. "For shame! Our father will hear of your treatment of her."

"Not before my father hears of your treachery. In this city, he has more friends than Ezra." Joiada spat out their father's name like a curse.

"What treachery could a young woman be involved in, may I ask?" Jarah asked dryly, rising to a height equal with the angry priest's.

"The same thing you're all involved in. Ezra wants to usurp my father's place as high priest. You're making his priestly robe. This child told me when I asked why she was carrying a length of purple cloth, the color of kings and priests."

"Our father doesn't want to be high priest. He wants to teach the people Torah," Hadassah said, her tone low and furious. "Did he hurt you?" she asked her whimpering sister. Adin shook her head.

"Then why the priestly robe to outshine my father?"

"How many robes do you see here?" Jarah gestured toward their work. "Let me help you since it appears you're not thinking clearly today. There are three—three!"

"I just told him about abba's, so I wouldn't spoil the surprise," Adin whispered. "I never thought he'd react like this."

"One's for your father, one's for my father. Would you like to guess who the third is for?" Hadassah asked.

"Her husband?" Joiada said, pointing to Jarah. "He's part of this too, isn't he?"

"My husband's only a Levite. Would you listen to us? There's no conspiracy," Jarah said.

"Our father has four daughters. There's no son to succeed him," Hadassah added.

Joiada's brow crinkled. "He could train whoever he picks out as husbands for you," he said, sounding less confident.

"Good grief, man, think like a priest and not a madman!" Jarah said, wishing she could shake him. "The third robe's for you."

Joiada recoiled and looked uncertain. "You're just saying that because I discovered you."

"If you don't believe us, go ask your wife. Adin borrowed an old robe from her so we could size the new one properly," Hadassah answered.

Joiada retreated through the door.

"And if you still want this robe, tell her to come get it and finish it for you. I'm not touching it again," Jarah growled. "And neither are Ezra's daughters."

Chapter 29

Benjamin admired his wife as she stomped grapes in the upper vat on their property, outshining every other woman in the vineyard. The entire town helped harvest because grapes needed to be picked as soon as they sweetened. He would pay each family in wine, a wineskin for each worker. The families were responsible for bringing their own skins.

The red liquid flow into the lower vat through a channel he had carved in the rock the first year he tended the vineyard. What a job that had been! It had taken every waking moment that he wasn't dressing the vines.

The wine would ferment in the lower vat for a week. Then he and Judith would pour it into the wineskins or jars provided by these workers. They would jar the rest. Next year they would start selling it. He had twenty pots from last year that he could sell in Jerusalem now that it had aged a year. Only two of last year's jars had turned to vinegar. He might even keep some of the wine to age for another year. Then it would bring even more at the market, or at the temple. They needed good wine for the sacrifices, and his was high quality since he never added water.

A flurry in the upper vat caught his attention. Ariel's pregnant wife had slipped on the skins and was struggling to rise. The petite woman was covered in crimson. Some of the women snickered behind their hands. Although her family's claim to the vineyard threatened his livelihood, he pitied her and started toward her to help. He doubted Judith would offer her a hand. His wife sometimes showed a harsh edge. Besides Tova, none of the women of Gibeon worked closely with her, but Judith was everything he wanted...and more.

He hoped they would have a daughter who looked like her mother. All Jews wished for a son, and he wanted a boy too, but not this time. He wanted a graceful girl with brown eyes.

Judith's alluring dark eyes had captured him when he met her more than three harvests ago. They held the promise of all sorts of pleasures she had more than delivered.

Before Benjamin could reach the floundering woman, Tova, huge with a child she could deliver any day, helped her regain her footing. What a good woman! It was a blessing for Judith to have such a friend.

Naama struggled not to cry as she thanked her rescuer. She could hear the suppressed laughter of the other women as she climbed out of the cubit-deep vat with Tova's support.

"Are you all right?" Tova asked anxiously.

"Except for my dignity," Naama said wryly. "Thank you again."

Tova must have read the question on Naama's face. Naama's grandmother had always said her face betrayed her thoughts. Usually a swat accompanied the words. "I was a newcomer not long ago. It gets easier. I want you to know you can count me as a friend. I'm going to be busy with this baby soon, but come by our home any time."

Naama stopped to see Tova within days. She had been working on a rug, which reminded her of her mother, so she decided to suppress her homesickness by visiting the one person who had reached out to her. *Maybe Jarah will arrive before the next new moon.*

As soon as she stepped into Tova's house, she realized her new friend was in labor. Tova was kneading her lower back as much as the dough she was preparing.

"How are you feeling?" Naama asked, questioning whether

Tova recognized these early signs.

"Pretty well. I feel like I can barely move these days." Tova gave her a rueful smile. "I wish Menachem had stayed home today. He's out hunting birds."

"Tova, my grandmother was the midwife for the Persian harem. My mother and I assisted her many times. I think your baby is on its way. Could I get the midwife for you?"

Tova regarded her with dawning understanding. "I have been feeling strangely since I woke up early with this pain in my back. Moving around seems to ease it some."

"Do whatever helps. I wish someone could be here with you while I fetch the midwife. Where does she live?"

"Not far. Go down this street toward the town's center and take the road going north. Dinah's the seventh house. I'll be fine while you're gone. Judith may come by soon."

It seemed to Tova that as soon as Naama disappeared through the doorway her back pain increased. *Probably because I know the child's coming.* Tova took a few deep breaths and moved to the sleeping mat she hadn't put away yet. *I think I'm ready to lie down for a bit.* As soon as she was down, she realized she wouldn't be able to rise without help. *Ah well, the midwife will be here soon. And I hope Naama returns with her.*

When she heard the sound of footsteps, the pain abated, but it wasn't the shuffling steps of the elderly midwife. Judith poked her head in the door.

"Tova, what's wrong? Why are you in bed? Is it time for the baby? Is Menachem getting the midwife?"

"No, he's hunting. Naama stopped by, told me I was in labor, and went to get Dinah," Tova answered between panting breaths.

Judith bustled over to the fire and stirred the embers. "I'll boil this water. When they get back, I'll fill these other water pots."

"I'm sorry. I didn't get to the spring this morning, and Menachem left early."

"Never mind. You've more important things to do today."

Naama burst through the door, acknowledging Judith with a nod. "Bad news. Dinah is burning with fever. Her son sent me to Carmela's house, but three of her children have fevers too. I told her it wouldn't be safe for her to come and bring the sickness here. That leaves us." She looked at Judith uncertainly, "Glad you're here. We're going to need as many hands as possible."

Tova almost laughed when Judith's mouth hung open, but she hurt too much. Judith detested the family that had claimed her vineyard. "Please, Judith," she whispered.

"I was just saying we need more water. I'll go get it," Judith said haughtily to Naama.

"Good." Naama turned her attention back to Tova, "Have you felt a rush of water yet?"

"No."

"May I feel your belly?"

"Yes. You'll have to be the midwife. Judith hasn't done this before." Tova bit her lip. "How many births have you attended?"

"Scores. I even delivered several babies on my own, for Jewish women in Susa," Naama answered with a soothing voice. "My grandmother had died, and my mother Artystone was helping other women. Seems like babies arrive in waves."

Tova detected a slight change in Naama's voice as she probed. "What is it?" she asked.

"I think the baby is lying with his face against your belly instead of facing your back. That's why you're having back pain."

Fear gripped Tova. "Will he be all right?"

"It won't hurt the baby," Naama assured her. "It just makes it difficult for you. And long. We need to convince this baby to turn."

"How?"

"Let's try getting you up on your hands and knees." Naama helped Tova move into position before she experienced another contraction. Since Judith had returned, Naama motioned for her to sit beside Tova and apply cool water to her face.

"How did that feel?"

"Not good, but better than before. I don't know how long I can stay like this."

"Let us know when you tire. We'll help you down onto your side or get you up to walk," Naama said.

"It's good that Menachem is off hunting," Judith commented.

"He doesn't even know the baby's coming." A tear trickled from Tova's eye.

"Your pains are far apart. He'll be back before your baby arrives," Naama said.

For the noon meal, Judith found barley bread and figs for herself and Naama. Tova refused the food but took frequent sips of water.

"Rock your hips back and forth. Maybe that will encourage this little one to cooperate," Naama encouraged.

"What if he doesn't turn?"

"Most babies turn, after causing their moms plenty of agony. A few are born face up. How long have you been having back pain?"

"She was rubbing it yesterday when I stopped by," Judith said, running her wet hand along her friend's brow and cheeks. "But she's been doing that since the baby got heavy."

"It did hurt more yesterday," Tova said. "I had to stop to rest more often, but I slept well most of the night. The ache woke me up early."

"You've probably been in labor for at least half a day," Naama mused.

"My mother had her babies quickly," Judith said. "One night I'd go to sleep, and in the morning my father would announce the birth of a new brother."

"My softa always said first babies take longer," Naama said, placing her hands on Tova's lower back. "I'm going to push a little. Let me know how it feels."

"That feels better. Keep doing it. Why does this have to hurt so much?" she panted, glistening with sweat.

"My mother told me blessings are often birthed through pain. Focus on the blessing—the little one you'll soon be holding."

∞∞∞

The women were all tired when Menachem and Benjamin returned around the time of the evening meal with four doves. When they strode into the room with the dead birds, Tova retched at the smell, and they retreated hastily. Judith joined her husband to pluck and roast the fowl. Menachem paced distractedly in the street at the front of his house.

They all cheered when Naama checked the baby's position again and announced he had turned. The labor pains increased in intensity and frequency until the second watch when the exhausted mother pushed one last time to deliver a tiny blue-faced baby.

Naama put her finger into the infant's mouth to dislodge any fluid. She turned him over and tapped his back. Then she held him on his side and reinserted her finger. She wiped the gunk on her robe and patted him again. The baby wheezed out a cry.

Naama continued to massage his tiny body while Judith cut the cord as she had been instructed earlier. Menachem held the swaddled baby by the warmth of the fire while Naama pushed on Tova's stomach to expel the afterbirth.

Tova whimpered.

"I know it's hard, and you want to hold your little boy, but this is really important. I need to make sure we get it all out, or you could sicken. You did a great job, Tova."

"Thank you for helping me."

"What's your son's name?" she asked when Menachem brought him to the new mother.

"Eliezer. It means 'God is my help,'" he replied.

Naama positioned the tiny boy at his mother's breast where he sucked weakly. *This baby is going to need all the help he can get.*

Chapter 30

T hat man needs his head examined," Jarah declared, shaking her head as she wove the shuttle in and out of the threads on her loom. Oren had constructed the wooden loom for her a few days after they had arrived in Jerusalem.

"I noticed his wife finished his robe," Hadassah said, standing to make red thread with a hand spindle. She lifted her right arm, smoothing the linen fibers with her left so the twisting action of the spindle would form thread. After Jarah had showed her the process and Hadassah had completed six spindles of plain white for everyday clothes, Jarah had declared her skillful enough to make fine thread for the priestly robe. "I bet Oren has never owned a robe of the quality we're making. I hope he appreciates his wife's skill."

"The quality of the cloth depends on the thread," Jarah answered. "Thank you for spinning it for me. My aunt and cousins made most of my thread so I could concentrate on the weaving. They did most of the sewing too."

"What did Joiada's wife say when she came to collect his partially finished robe?"

"Not much. She inspected the sewing and seemed impressed with the work. She said she would finish it, so I could work on the other robes."

"Do you think Joiada told her about collaring Adin?"

"I doubt it. That would require some shred of humility," Jarah said. "I'm not sure he even mentioned that you and your sisters were helping me. She seemed to think I was working alone."

"Abba humbled him. When I told abba about that man touching Adin, he made sure Adin was unharmed and then stormed out with his fists clenched. I've never seen him so angry. Not much later he came back with Joiada, and Joiada apologized.

"I don't think he was sorry. He didn't bother to apologize when it happened. What's wrong with him?"

"He wants power," Hadassah said sadly. "I thought I was escaping the pressure of power struggles when I left the palace. How could anyone think abba wants to become high priest? He's a teacher."

"Some men are threatened by anything, and your father does share the lineage of the high priest and his family."

"It seems like more than that. Do you think he's hiding something?"

Joiada shifted restlessly as he listened to Ezra convince his father and a council of priests that bet 'ammas would benefit the people. "The prophet Ezekiel began them after the Babylonians took us captive. The exiles needed God's words desperately, and these houses of the people sprouted up throughout Babylon and Persia."

"Who teaches God's words?" Meremoth questioned.

"Three men read portions of Torah. Then they offer comments."

"But what if they misunderstand or misinterpret the passage?" a white-bearded priest asked.

"All the men discuss the passages after the service ends. The comments aren't the main reason people meet. They come to hear God's powerful, life-giving words. The comments enhance and explain the Torah. Everyone understands they're a man's interpretation, except if a prophet announces 'This is what the Lord says.'"

"Like Ezekiel," Meremoth said.

"Exactly."

"I have noticed the young men who returned with you know

the Torah and writings better than many of the priests," Eliashib said.

"I taught them every Sabbath during our trek, but some of them already had a good grasp of God's word. At the large bet 'ammas, the boys are taught the holy writings for seven years, beginning around the age of six. By the time they become men, they can recite long portions from memory. The best students go on to study and become the next generation of teachers."

"Impressive," Eliashib said, stroking his beard.

"That's fine for those who are still in Persia, but now every son of Israel in Yehud can worship at the temple," Joiada offered.

"Not every Jew can leave his work to travel to the temple each week. We must gather for the major celebrations, but we can't teach the people all they need to know, even at a week-long celebration like Passover."

"Israel's troubles began when King Jeroboam let the northern sons of Israel worship in Bethel," Joiada pointed out.

"He made an idol for them to worship and encouraged them to travel to Bethel for all the holy days, rather than to Jerusalem. The leaders of every bet 'amma will instruct their members to come to the temple to celebrate the Day of Atonement, Feast of Tabernacles, and Passover. And there will be no idols."

"We need to consider this carefully," Eliashib said.

Joiada studied Ezra's face and noticed a slight look of displeasure before Ezra nodded consent.

Chapter 31

In spite of her absorption in her wedding plans, Miriam noticed her sister's sober mood. "Do you know what's wrong with Hadassah?" she asked Adin.

"You're leaving."

"Hadassah will still have you and abba. And Rebekah's not far."

"But she's experienced loss after loss—Jedidiah, the queen, and now you."

"How did you become so wise, little sister?"

Adin smiled faintly. "Queen Esther said I'm sensitive because of my early losses."

Miriam nodded, thinking of Adin's twin who had died as a baby during the battle of Purim. Their mother Rachel died a couple years later. The twins' birth had been difficult, and she never recovered her strength. "A hard way to come by your gift."

"It was long ago. I am content with what Adonai has given me. After all, I have more than enough sisters," Adin responded, with a twinkle in her eye.

Hadassah caught the last comment as she entered the chamber. "You can never have too many, but I have the best."

"Well said. Let's spend the day together. I've been wanting to explore the walls," Miriam suggested.

Hadassah and Adin looked at each other. Poking through the tumbled walls sounded like one of Miriam's escapades. It appealed to neither of them.

"I suppose we should humor her," Adin said. "She is getting married. Rebekah would say her time to play is short."

"Go see if Rebekah can join us. I'll mix tonight's bread. Tell her

I'll make enough for her family too," Hadassah said to Adin.

"I'll refill the water pot," Miriam offered.

∞∞∞

Hadassah shaded her eyes and watched her three younger sisters climb on the ruined walls, which must have been formidable in the days before the Babylonians toppled them.

Miriam leaped from stone to stone. Rebekah climbed around them, testing her footing at every step. Adin stayed on the ground and skirted the ruins while keeping up with the other two. Hadassah stuck to the travel-worn path that avoided the rubble but followed the circumference of the city.

Rebekah's caution troubled Hadassah. Her second sister usually dared as much as Miriam. It was a mercy they hadn't both been killed after their mother died and their father barely went through the motions of living. Since Hadassah had been waiting on the queen since the age of five, she hadn't taken care of them. The Jewish community in Susa returned Miriam and Rebekah to their father every time they wandered off, which was a frequent occurrence. Hadassah suspected kind neighbors fed the girls around noon since their father forgot. A young widow who lived on their street had cared for Adin, who liked to stay close to home. It was a good thing since she was only a toddler. She might have been crushed by a cart if she had run around like the other two.

But why was Rebekah moving so cautiously now? She didn't seem the same woman since she married. Was her husband disappointing her, or mistreating her? Or maybe she was expecting a child?

Hadassah lazed along, enjoying the meager warmth of the sun, grateful the rains had paused. A shriek and sound of scraping stone roused her. Except for Adin, her sisters had disappeared from view due to the tumbled rock wall. As she caught up, she saw Miriam balanced on a piece of wall the size of six camels.

"Move backward," Rebekah urged.

"I'm afraid to," Miriam answered.

"The rock won't shift if you move back. I can see how it's perched on a jagged stone. It's only unstable if you move forward."

Slowly, Miriam shifted one foot back. Finding solid footing, she moved her other foot. After several baby steps, she hitched up her skirt and leaped to the rock Rebekah stood on.

"That was close," Rebekah said, hugging her. "If you'd been farther forward, the entire slab would have tipped."

"And likely have crushed you," Hadassah added, grabbing both sisters as they returned to solid ground. "Enough adventure for today. Let's go finish tonight's meal."

Even Miriam didn't argue as the sisters linked arms and turned toward the temple.

Chapter 32

Miriam twirled on bare feet in her bridal gown. Hadassah smiled at her sister's enthusiasm. Adin scooted back from snipping loose threads in the border of lilies. The cloth was blue silk, purchased in Susa. Miriam had added the border with gold thread, refusing to marry until it was completed.

Why would a bride delay her wedding? Hadassah would have married Jedidiah in any garment she owned, but Queen Esther had commissioned a scarlet dress and robe and clasped a gold necklace around her neck right before the groomsmen arrived to escort her to the wedding. She said the ensemble was her gift to the bride.

Ezra had married them in the private courtyard owned by Jedidiah's family. Hadassah could still smell the fragrance of the blossoming citrus trees. She shook off her memories. Tonight was Miriam's wedding. After three days of celebration, she would be leaving them for Gibeon, where the groom's family had reclaimed their property.

Hadassah liked Miriam's groom. Miriam and Samuel had known each other since they were children. In fact, Samuel was the son of Amaris, one of their mother's closest friends. After Rachel died, Amaris mothered Rebekah, Miriam, and Adin as much as her own lively brood would allow. She didn't have much time while caring for her own six children, but she had won the girls' confidence. Miriam would gain a caring mother along with a husband tonight. Hadassah's heart ached a little as she adjusted the veil concealing Miriam's face. The sounds of shofars and singing reached their ears. The groomsmen were coming, announcing the wedding on rams' horns.

Miriam fingered the beaten-gold amulets hanging on a gold chain around her neck, her gift from the groom. Hadassah realized with amusement that her irrepressible younger sister was nervous.

"You're always beautiful, Miriam, but today you..." Hadassah's voice broke.

"...outshine the stars," Adin finished with a look of awe.

Miriam looped an arm around each of them. "Come see us. Come see us soon, especially you, Hadassah. Since we'll be living in Gibeon, you'd be able to see Jarah and Naama too."

Hadassah nodded. She would go visit, but she would wait, give the newlyweds time. Miriam didn't realize how the days would slip away like fine sand in an hour glass. Hadassah intended to wait a year before visiting. Perhaps in a year's time there would be a baby she could tend.

The men arrived at the door while Miriam's female friends lifted oil lamps to surround the house with light. Miriam took a deep breath. Adin opened the door with a flourish to reveal Samuel, garbed in a white robe, offering Miriam his hand. As soon as she accepted it, the couple was swept into the throng of well-wishers. They escorted her to his uncle's fine house in Jerusalem, and Ezra pronounced the ceremonial blessings over wine brought from Gibeon. Miriam circled her groom seven times, and the two retired to the wedding chamber prepared by the groom.

Hadassah and Jarah sat quietly together on a stone bench, sipping wine and waiting for the announcement of consummation from the bridal chamber. Then the feasting would begin. Hadassah hoped her younger sister would enjoy her night. She had tried to prepare Miriam for the marriage bed, as Queen Esther had instructed her before her wedding night.

Jedidiah had been gentle and kind, as he was in everything. Their wedding week had been blissful.

Hadassah paused on the opposite side of the temple from their chambers. Her father would not come home after the day's revelations, but perhaps she could get him to eat something. She had brought unleavened bread and lamb stew. Since Ezra wasn't in the chamber, she put the food on a table and followed the crowd.

She had heard mourning cries all day from a growing number of Israelites who congregated inside the temple and spilled over into the streets. Adin had stopped sewing and gone to investigate the problem. She didn't return, but Hadassah wasn't particularly curious. She needed to keep busy, so she baked bread, pounding the dough over and over. It was a miracle she hadn't over-kneaded them, but at the end of the day she had eight golden brown loaves.

The throng was too large for her to see what was going on, but she found Jarah near the back and got an explanation from her. "Meremoth and a delegation of priests and leaders approached your father after the morning sacrifice. Oren was nearby, and he told me what they said. 'The people of Israel and the priests and Levites have not separated themselves from the peoples of the land. They have taken some of their daughters as wives for themselves and their sons. The leaders and rulers have been the worst offenders.' Your father ripped his robe and has been sitting in front of the altar, speechless. The people have been gathering all day to hear his verdict."

Hadassah offered a prayer for wisdom for her father. These marriages with pagans were a serious breach of God's law. While in captivity, the Jews had kept their identity as a people by marrying among themselves. Few married Babylonians or Persians, with the exception of proselytes like Naama. If the Jews married into the surrounding nations, they would essentially cease to exist as a people.

Movement rippled through the crowd, and priests brought the sacrificial lamb, but Ezra, in a voice that carried to the back of the crowd, called, "Halt. Let us confess our sin, or these sacrifices will mean nothing to our God."

Ezra rose from the ground but did not lift his face and hands in the customary gestures of prayer. Instead he stared at the ground. "'O my God, I am too ashamed and humiliated to lift up my face to you, my God; for our iniquities have risen higher than our heads, and our guilt has grown up to the heavens. Since the days of our fathers to this day we have been very guilty, and for our iniquities we, our kings, and our priests have been delivered into the hand of the kings of the lands, to the sword, to captivity, to plunder, and to humiliation, as it is this day.'"

Hadassah heard her father's shuddering sigh as he continued: "'And now for a little while grace has been shown from the Lord our God, to leave us a remnant to escape, and to give us a peg in His holy place, that our God may enlighten our eyes and give us a measure of revival in our bondage. For we were slaves. Yet our God did not forsake us in our bondage, but extended mercy to us in the sight of the kings of Persia, to revive us, to repair the house of our God, to rebuild its ruins, and to give us a wall in Judah and Jerusalem.

"'And now, O our God, what shall we say after this? For we have forsaken your commandments, which you commanded by your servants the prophets, saying, "The land which you are entering to possess is an unclean land, with the uncleanness of the peoples of the lands, with their abominations which have filled it from one end to another with their impurity. Now therefore, do not give your daughters as wives for their sons, nor take their daughters to your sons; and never seek their peace or prosperity, that you may be strong and eat the good of the land, and leave it as an inheritance to your children forever.

"'And after all that has come upon us for our evil deeds and for our great guilt, since You our God have punished us less than our iniquities deserve, and have given us such deliverance as this, should we again break Your commandments, and join in marriage with the people committing these abominations?'" Ezra's voice rose. "'Would You not be angry with us until You had consumed us, so that there would be no remnant or survivor? O Lord God of Israel, You are righteous, for we are left as a remnant. Here we are before You, in our guilt, though no one can stand before You because of this!'"

The wails of the humbled Jews filled the temple courtyards. The grief was not the formal wailing of a funeral. Grown men were sobbing openly beside their weeping wives. The children cried pathetically, uncomprehending but frightened by the adults' reaction.

A loud bass voice rumbled over the waves of sorrow. "We have sinned against our gracious God and taken pagan wives, but there is still hope. Let's divorce these wives and put away their children and follow God's law. Ezra, take this responsibility and help us. We are with you."

Hadassah looked for the source of the voice and saw a path open in the crowd. Now she could see her father. An older Jew walked steadily towards him.

"You have spoken wisely, Shecaniah," Ezra answered. He turned to the crowd. "Are the rest of you agreed?"

The crowd roared, "Yes," with one voice.

"Will you swear it?"

The leaders bowed and nodded, and all the people said, "Amen."

"Then may our gracious God spare us. Summon all Israel to this place in three days' time. If any refuses to come, confiscate his property and cut him off from Israel."

After the evening sacrifice was made, Ezra retired to Johanan's chamber. The crowd quieted and returned to their homes while chosen messengers sped to the corners of Israel.

Chapter 33

Naama watched from the door of their stone hut as her family, the elders, and Benjamin set boundary stones in place. The allotted piece looked far too small to support them, but last night the elders said if they would renounce their alleged rights to the portion cultivated by Benjamin, he would never challenge their right to the rest.

Gili was furious, but Ariel had pointed out, "We're the outsiders here. If the Ammonite family had still owned it, we might have been able to appeal to Ezra, but a Jew with deep family roots in Gibeon has owned it for several years. What can we do?"

Gili had stalked off to cool his temper.

Just as she turned to re-enter her small home, she heard screaming. Judith appeared through the vines, calling the men pigs, and worse. She was a beautiful woman, even with her face twisted in anger.

Naama didn't blame her for being angry. The entire vineyard had been her dowry, passed down through her family for generations. The vines left to her family would support them, but not abundantly. For the thousandth time, Naama wished they had stayed in Susa.

Benjamin quickly took his wife by the hand and bundled her back into their cottage, hushing her cries. As they disappeared, a man came up the muddy path on a horse.

"Shalom. I was told in the village that all the elders were out in Benjamin's vineyard. Have I found the right place?"

The elders greeted him politely and assured him of their identities.

"I bear a message from Ezra that all Israelites gather at the temple in two days. Any who refuses to come will forfeit his property and be cut off from Israel."

"Come to the gate with us, brother, and tell us everything," said the most wizened of the men, leaning on his walking stick.

"I have to keep traveling to spread the word. Two days isn't a lot of time. Ezra will explain it all to you. Shalom."

The men looked at each other in puzzlement. Hastily they set a couple more stones before racing back to the village to find out if anyone had more information.

∞∞∞

"But, Ariel, I can't possibly make the trip up to Jerusalem now. The baby will be coming soon," Naama said.

"Ezra has called for every Israelite to present himself in Jerusalem, or he forfeits his property and citizenship," Ariel answered.

"I'm sure the great Ezra will exempt me," Naama answered dryly.

"He has to make some concessions for the pregnant, old, or sick," Gili said. "Still . . . we've just regained some of our land. Are you sure you can't make the trip? You could ride the donkey."

Naama glared at both men. "I'm huge. I can barely make it to the spring. I have to stop two or three times on the steps down to the water. Getting up is worse. As for riding a donkey, all that up and down would probably send me into early labor. Is that what you want?" She felt like shouting "I'm not going anywhere," but clamped her mouth shut as tears started.

Men are infuriating! Let one of them try carrying a child for just one week and see if they make these ridiculous suggestions. She turned her back on them and stirred the soup while listening to the rain pattering on the roof. She was so thankful for that roof, and now they wanted her to leave its shelter and make a long trip *in her condition*!

The men noticed the sound of the rain too. "It's not good

weather for traveling," Gili noted. "And Ezra's daughter Hadassah can vouch for Naama's condition."

"I can't force her to travel right now. It could be disastrous, and I'd never forgive myself." Ariel moved to Naama's side and reached around her girth. "It will be all right, *matok*. The most important thing is your life and the life of our child. Surely the elders of our town can understand."

"And we'll draw several days of water for you before we go," Gili added.

Now that's more like it, Naama thought, swiping at her eyes with the back of her hand.

∞∞∞

"Should we travel with such a frail baby?" Tova asked as she and Menachem considered their son Eliezer. "He's finally getting bigger, but he didn't have a good start."

She had tended him exclusively for three moons, nursing him almost continually. She had accomplished nothing around their home, but she had managed to keep their firstborn alive.

Menachem had little work at this time of year, so he fetched the water and ground the flour. The village women kindly baked it for them since Menachem's first and only attempt had resulted in a charred mess and flames that nearly burned everything in their stone house. Tova managed to make a lentil soup every few days. Otherwise, she rested and cared for Eliezer. And, finally, Eliezer was growing more and fussing less.

"I'm worried for you if we don't make the trip," Menachem said. "I know you love and serve Adonai, the One True God. But the rumors say many Ammonite women will be divorced. The leaders may consider your pagan heritage more than your pure heart, matok. That would be disastrous for you *and* Eliezer."

He paced the small room. "We need to make this trip together. We will pray and trust Adonai to continue to strengthen our son."

Chapter 34

Tova felt like lying down in the mud and never getting up again. She was tired and miserable from the wet day's travel to Jerusalem. Eliezer was wailing for his dinner, but they couldn't find a place to stay the night.

"Let's eat at this inn and get warm by the fire. I'll find a dry room for you afterwards, Tova."

Tova strongly suspected all the dry rooms in Jerusalem were taken, but she gratefully stepped into the warmth of this inn. She unwrapped Eliezer from layers of blankets and was relieved to find his chest and hands warm. Of course he was wet farther down because she hadn't changed him for hours. Their group had been trying to make it to the city before darkness settled and the roads became more dangerous. Blessed be Adonai, they had achieved that goal. She was concerned about where they would sleep, but the heat seeping into her bones restored her perspective. They had reached Jerusalem safely!

Menachem found her a spot near the fire where she could suckle their son and stood in front of them protectively. He ordered two portions of goat and bread, which were ready by the time Eliezer contentedly drifted to sleep. Tova swaddled him in a dry blanket and settled down to eat hungrily. When she finished, she found Menachem studying her.

"I'll go ask the inn keeper if he knows of any empty lodgings, Tova. Wait here."

Tova felt the good meal sit like a stone in her stomach. *Will we have to camp outside in the downpour with Eliezer?* Many Gibeonites stayed with family in the city, but Menachem had no relatives here.

She nodded and settled herself in the corner with Eliezer in her arms.

∞∞∞∞

Oren came into their small room and shook a puddle of water onto the stone floor. Jarah smiled warmly at him and hung his cloak to dry. She removed the cooking pot from its place over the fire and set it on the hearth. When she finished, she crouched on a stool close to the fire and watched her husband. He was looking around their room, as if measuring it. She had never seen him study their chamber so intently. He approached the hearth slowly, without his usual alacrity to inhale dinner.

"Is everything all right, Oren?"

"Well... I met someone out in the rain. He needed help, and I offered it, but now that I see how small our place is, I'm not sure."

"What kind of help does he need?"

"He needs shelter for his wife and baby. I overheard him praying. It was a heartfelt prayer, Jarah. He was *talking* to the Most High, not stringing together lofty words. I hear many worshippers *saying* prayers, but with this man, I could tell he was conversing with Adonai. And he was desperate. So I thought, maybe the Most High wanted to use me to provide the answer to this prayer. I offered him and his family a place to stay for the night, but now I see how cramped we'll be." His voice drifted off as his wife jumped up and ran to the door.

"Where are they?" she asked as she peered out into the rainy night. "Of course they must come in!"

Oren laughed as he closed the door. "I'm relieved to hear you say that, Jarah. You have a big heart."

"You're the one who invited them in the first place. But where are they?"

"He left his wife and child at the inn where they ate dinner. I showed him which chamber is ours, and he went to fetch them."

"Let's eat quickly. Then I'll go see if Hadassah has extra blankets to make up a pallet near the fire since theirs are probably wet. If not, we'll share. Imagine--traveling in this weather with a baby!"

Chapter 35

The next day dawned rainy. Oren left to fulfill his duties, and soon after, Menachem joined the crowd of men in the courtyard.

Tova fed Eliezer while Jarah straightened the chamber.

"I've never visited Jerusalem before," Tova said.

"It's too bad it's raining. Otherwise I could show you around. It's a charming old city," Jarah answered.

Having only seen the wall's rubble and a few muddy streets through the lens of weariness, Tova was inclined to disagree. "At least I'll get to see some of the temple later. We need to make the sacrifice for Eliezer."

"Why did you wait this long?" popped out of Jarah's mouth before she could stop it.

Tova didn't seem offended. She turned Eliezer and held him up for Jarah to view. "He looks healthy now, but we almost lost him at birth. He wasn't breathing. My neighbor managed to rub some life into him, but he's always sucked weakly, until lately, that is."

"I'd never have guessed. You've taken great care of him, Tova. I'm sure that will be taken into account."

"What do you mean?"

"You're an Ammonite, aren't you? Menachem said you were last night."

"Yes."

"The priests will want to know what delayed the sacrifice for your firstborn. You have a good explanation and have obviously cared for this little son of Israel splendidly. I don't think the delay will count against you."

"I hope not. I hadn't considered how it would look to people who don't know us. Everyone in our village knows what's been happening. They've been helping Menachem so I could take care of Eliezer. He needed to eat constantly."

Regretting her thoughtlessness, Jarah took Tova's hands in her own, "I'm an orphan, Tova. And I just married Oren though I'm years older than you. Adonai has always watched over me even when I didn't think He remembered me. Do you know the words of the prophet Isaiah? I think they're made for you right now because I can see how much you love your son. 'Can a mother forget the baby at her breast and have no compassion on the child she has borne? Though she may forget, I will not forget you. See, I have engraved you on the palms of my hands.'"

"So the God of Israel loves me even more than I love Eliezer?" Tova gazed into her baby's face. "I've never heard those words. Obviously I didn't grow up in a family who worshipped the one true God. I didn't know much about Adonai until I met Menachem. He's taught me a little, but…"

"That's why Rabbi Ezra came back to Yehud—to teach the people God's ways. Back in Babylon, we went to bet 'amma's every Sabbath to hear the scrolls and be taught from them. Ezra plans to start one in every village."

"I hope so! Eliezer can learn from the time he's a child. That would be the best way. It's hard to change old ways of thinking. Many of the Ammonite women haven't been able to."

"If they had chosen Adonai like you, He would have helped them."

"And now it's too late," Tova said with tears in her eyes, thinking of Judith.

"For some, but not for you," Jarah said firmly.

After Jarah started some bread and set it aside to rise, she asked hesitantly, "Could I hold him?"

Tova laughed. "Absolutely. I was just wondering how I could go outside and hear what's going on without exposing him to the rain. Unless you want to go," she added quickly.

"I'd rather sit by the fire and admire Eliezer. Oren will fill me in later."

Tova handed Jarah the baby and donned her hooded cloak.

∞∞∞∞

When Tova reached the back of the silent crowd, she could hear Ezra clearly. He condemned the Jews' intermarriages and urged them to confess their sin and divorce their wives.

She searched the crowd, trying to locate Menachem in the crush. Most of the crowd consisted of men, but women and children were present too. Tova read terror in some of the women's faces. She finally spied a group of men from Gibeon, including her husband. She couldn't see his face. Benjamin was shifting nervously on his feet, drawing irritated looks from those around him.

The crowd began to shout their agreement. "That's right. This is our duty. We will do as you say." Tova noticed Benjamin wasn't shouting with the rest of his countrymen but could only glimpse Menachem's back. She shivered.

The crowd began milling around, and the hum of subdued voices filled the air. A score of women from Moab and Ammon swept out of the courtyard, faces proud and heads held high. Other women remained behind, faces stricken and tear-stained.

A ram's horn blew to restore the people's attention to Ezra.

"It's raining and many of you have sinned, so we won't stay until these matters are resolved. In each town, the elders will consider the cases of intermarriage and decide which need to be dissolved. At set times, the elders and guilty men will return here before me and the priests to finalize the divorces and resolve any lingering conflicts. Go in peace to do the will of our God."

Tova felt immense relief. *The men of Gibeon know I serve Adonai. They won't force Menachem to divorce me, will they?*

Menachem found her walking back to Oren's chamber. Nei-

141

ther wanted to voice their concerns, so Menachem chose a safer subject. "Oren said it would be easier to offer our sacrifice in the afternoon, after most of the people have left. He said it's too late for us to start back to Gibeon now and invited us to stay for another night." Menachem eyed his wife anxiously. "Let's ask Jarah the best place to buy turtle doves. We can explore the city a little before we buy them, but you'll still have time for a rest before the sacrifice."

"That sounds wonderful," Tova said, appreciating his thoughtfulness for her and their son. "What can we do to thank Jarah and Oren for their hospitality?"

"I have no idea. We'll look for something when we reach the marketplace."

When they entered the small room and found Jarah rocking their baby by the fire, Tova immediately knew the desire of Jarah's heart. But it was beyond her power to give.

Chapter 36

After Tova's family left, Jarah missed having another woman to talk to as she did chores, so she gathered a robe in need of hemming and went in search of Hadassah. The rain and mud would keep them indoors, but it was better than being confined to her room by herself.

I want to worship at the temple every day, but I'm tired of our little room. I can't wait to see Oren's family's house and check on Naama. I can continue my work in Gibeon.

She, Hadassah and Adin had completed five priestly robes, actually four and a half since Joiada's wife finished his. The priests needed white linen tunics, but she and Hadassah decided to fashion the robes first since they would hide the shabby tunics. Jarah hoped the priests' wives would decide to make their husbands' tunics. Of course, a few priests were losing their wives because they had married foreign women. She and her friends would have to sew theirs.

Looming the material and cutting and sewing priestly robes and tunics would give her work for years. By the time she finished, the first robes would need mending or replacing. Jarah was thrilled to use her skills for Adonai's temple, and Ezra had paid her two silver coins for the first five robes. Hadassah and her sisters each earned one. With her coins, Jarah bought a lamb they sacrificed the next day.

I've finished everything I wanted to accomplish here in Jerusalem. We'll leave soon, but be back in six moons for Oren to serve again.

When Jarah knocked, Hadassah answered and quickly drew her into the main room. Due to Ezra's importance and larger family, they lived in three rooms with connecting doors. The middle room served as the kitchen and family gathering place. Ezra's sleeping mat and scrolls filled a small room to the right, and Hadassah and her sisters slept in the larger bedroom to the left. A small fire kept the chill from the room without heating it too much.

"I know what he was hiding," Hadassah announced.

"Who's hiding?" Jarah asked in confusion.

"Joiada. Remember I thought he was hiding something?"

"Yes."

"His brother-in-law is married to a Moabite."

"Oh!"

"That's not all. They have a son."

Jarah digested that information. "He'll be sent away with his mother?"

"Yes, but his father's been bringing him into the temple."

Jarah didn't understand the significance.

"Moabites aren't allowed into the temple until the sixth generation," Hadassah explained. "The family is disgraced, which also affects Joiada, because he married one of their daughters."

"Does that affect his birthright as the firstborn son of the high priest?"

"I don't know, but Joiada's probably nervous about it."

Chapter 37

After the tiresome trip home, Tova longed for a good night's rest, but as soon as they lay down, someone pounded on the door. Menachem grunted and rose, wrapping his cloak around himself and exiting the one-room hut. He called for Tova to come quickly.

When Tova emerged from the warmth of their home into the cold, damp night, Benjamin's wild look told her all she needed to know. "The baby's coming?"

He nodded wordlessly. Menachem gathered a sleeping Eliezer, and they began to walk out to the vineyard. Tova hoped Judith was more collected than her husband and that Benjamin had already fetched the midwife.

To her relief, the midwife had arrived and was handing Judith a skin of water when Tova entered the two-room hut. And, other than a white face, Judith seemed to be doing well.

"The pains are close together. She's been doing a fine job," the midwife said as Tova entered.

Tova smiled at her friend.

Soon Judith was rocking on hands and knees. Tova wiped her brow with a cool cloth and murmured encouragement.

The midwife said, "When you feel the need to push, tell me. I'll check the baby first. We have to keep the cord out of the way. This shouldn't take much longer."

Moments later Judith yelled that she needed to push. The elderly midwife said to wait and probed with her fingers around the baby's neck. Then she gave the signal to push.

Judith pushed only a few times before the baby's head emerged. Tova caught the child and held her while the midwife cut the cord. "She's beautiful, Judith. Let me clean her off," Tova said, holding the baby where Judith could see.

"It's a girl?" Judith sounded disappointed.

"Yes. She's perfect."

Judith closed her eyes and a few drops trickled down her cheeks. Tova thought she heard Judith whisper, "It's all over" as she laid the little girl on her mother's chest.

"The midwife's going to wait for the after-birth and clean you up, but the hard part's over. You were so much braver than I."

"Your labor was longer. And you did better than Menachem. He nearly passed out."

"Benjamin didn't look good when he got to our house. He's outside with Menachem and Eliezer. I'll go tell him the good news."

∞∞∞

The next day Tova returned with unleavened bread and a jug of water. "I'm baking more bread to bring over later. It's not ready, so I brought this."

"Thank you," Judith answered.

"Did you name your little girl?"

"Benjamin said he wants to name her Hen because he's sure she'll have all her mother's charm and grace." Judith looked at her baby. "She *is* a pretty little thing. Lucky for me she's small. I think her size made the delivery faster."

"Isn't Benjamin wonderful?" Tova asked, leaning over to admire the infant.

Judith hesitated. "Did he seem disappointed when you told him he had a daughter?"

"Not at all. You should have seen his relief when I told him you were fine and the baby was healthy. He was thrilled. You can have a son next time."

Judith didn't respond, and Tova saw sadness in her eyes.

Chapter 38

I t's time to go home." Oren swung his bride in an arc in the small chamber. Jarah felt her toes brush the walls.

"Put me down, Oren. I need to finish packing," she laughed. "No one's swung me around like a child since, well . . . I was a child."

"You're not a child?" he asked in mock disbelief. He tickled her waist, causing her to giggle. "You sound like one to me. And you liven things up like a child. Just what I need."

Jarah thrust a bundle into his hands. "Here, take this and the bedding near the door and start loading the donkey."

Oren stayed where he was. "I was going to ride, and let you carry the load," he teased.

Jarah put her hands on her hips and tried to look stern, but she dissolved into peals of laughter at the picture of their diminutive donkey topped by her husband, his feet dragging on the ground.

∞∞∞∞

"It was neighborly of Ariel and Gili to mend the roof of our home," Jarah said as the couple ate roasted grain while their donkey rested at midday.

"It was. I suspect they're trading their labor for your help when Naama's time comes."

"She said there's a midwife in Gibeon. I don't need skill, just the willingness to follow her directions."

"It will be good for the girl to have a familiar face. You said she misses her em."

"Yes. But her mother's skill and knowledge would have comforted her more than I ever could."

"I thought her mother was a rug maker."

"She is, but her grandmother Nasha was a midwife. She delivered babies at the palace, and her mother Artystone helped at many births."

"Her softa is dead?"

"Yes, but of natural causes. King Xerxes didn't execute her as he did her predecessor."

"Ayy, kings."

"Do you think Israel will ever have another king?"

Oren took his time to answer. "Not anytime soon. We're too weak to gain our freedom and choose a king, and the Persians won't appoint one. They appoint satraps and governors. It's more peaceful. Kings get ideas about making their own decisions and refusing to pay taxes. But someday…someday I believe there will be a King, a strong king to deliver us from foreign domination, a righteous king to reign with justice. That's one thing Ezra said in his daily teaching when he taught from the prophet Isaiah."

"I wish I could have heard his words."

"We have many rainy nights ahead. I'll tell you all I remember. By the time we have sons, we will have a bet 'amma, so all can learn."

"Like when we lived in Susa. Will the women be able to go, too?"

"On the Sabbath, we'll all go. And the other days, the boys will learn lessons for several hours, except during the harvest. Never again will the sons of Jacob forget the laws of the Most High. We will learn to recite them from our childhood."

"Marvelous!"

Oren's crooked grin foretold more news. "And Ezra wants me to be the teacher!"

"When did you find out? Why haven't you told me? Of course you must!"

"Whoa!" he lifted his hands to ward off the barrage of questions. "I haven't been keeping it secret. He told me yesterday when he realized my time at the temple had ended. Since then we've been busy getting ready to depart." Oren paused, "This means I'll need to spend more time at the temple than the other Levites."

Jarah nibbled on her bottom lip, considering the additional separations. "You still must do it. It's the right thing. And what an honor!"

Oren hugged her, praising Adonai for his understanding wife.

Chapter 39

J arah surveyed her spacious new home as she returned from Gibeon's well. It had three rooms downstairs and would have two above when they needed the space and Oren had time to build. Ariel and Gili had repaired the ceiling of the first floor. They had replaced eight wooden beams and layered twigs and limestone to withstand the winter rains. Their work would serve as a good foundation when the time came to rebuild the second story.

The wooden door opened into a narrow hall which Jarah would brighten with a tan and white weaving laced with red. Two rooms of the same length ran on either side of the hall. Both were more than twice as wide as the hall and boasted two small windows. The one to the right housed a large fireplace, table, and benches. The left chamber served as space for Jarah's loom and storage.

The newlyweds kept their sleeping mats in the large back room on a raised sleeping platform that ran the length of the house. Previous owners had reared many children here.

The back room also housed the remnants of a corral. Oren said they must have brought the sheep and goats in, especially during lambing season. Jarah regarded him in dismay.

"Don't worry. The donkey will stay outside in a shed I plan to build for our animals and my tools. I don't want to raise sheep. We'll be going back and forth from Jerusalem too often. I want you to come with me, at least until Adonai blesses us with children." Catching her expression, Oren added, "And he will. Have a little faith. How many moons have we been married?"

"Ten." Jarah had been keeping careful count, feeling disappointed every month.

"If Adonai chooses only to bless me with you, Jarah, I am a happy man. But think of Sarah, Rebekah, and Hannah. They all waited for their sons, and when the time was right, Adonai gave them very important babies."

"I know Sarah gave birth to Isaac, and Rebekah had the twins Jacob and Esau, but who is Hannah?"

"Have you heard of the prophet Samuel?"

"Just his name."

"Hannah was his mother. She promised Adonai that if he would give her a son the boy would be a Nazarite, dedicated to the Most High. As a young child, he served in the tabernacle and later delivered Israel from the Philistines. Eventually he anointed King Saul, and then King David."

"He wrote much of the history of Israel, didn't he?"

"Yes. I will tell you more of him tonight. Now I must meet with the village elders and deliver Ezra's instructions."

"And I will check on Naama."

"May the face of Adonai shine on you."

"And on you, husband."

"It's good we arrived when we did. Naama will deliver any day now. She doesn't look healthy to me, and she says she's been having trouble eating and sleeping. The midwife says the baby will come when he's ready, but Naama thinks he's late," Jarah reported later as the couple ate their bread and washed it down with new wine. "A big baby could lead to a difficult delivery."

"Is the bread sweetened tonight? Are we celebrating something?" Oren asked.

Jarah beamed. "Yes. You noticed. We're celebrating God's goodness in giving us this home, your family home. And thank you for braving those bees and collecting their honey."

"It was nothing. I was awake early so walked back to the

honey log we saw on our way into town a few days ago. Since it was still cool the bees were quiet."

"So tell me about Samuel and his mother."

"Hannah was one of the wives of a man named Elkanah. His other wife had more than one child and plagued Hannah unmercifully about her barrenness. Hannah wanted a son more than anything in the world, so on one of the family's trips to worship at the tabernacle she promised Adonai that if He would grant her a son, she would give him back all the days of his life. She vowed he would be a Nazarite."

"What's a Nazarite?"

"A man who drinks no wine, never cuts his hair, and refuses to touch the dead."

"That's not so bad."

"But Hannah meant she would also give him to God to serve at the tabernacle."

"So she would rarely see him."

"Exactly. It was her sacrifice."

"So the Most High gave her Samuel, which means gift of Adonai."

"Yes."

"And when he became a man, she sent him to the tabernacle?"

"No. When she weaned him."

"When she weaned him! But he would have been a little boy!"

"She fulfilled her vow, and he became a judge over all Israel."

"A son any mother would be proud of."

"Definitely."

As Jarah lay down to sleep, she pondered Hannah's vow and the sacrifice that followed. Should she promise Adonai something similar? But surely Oren would want a say! Elkanah already had children, so Hannah's son would not have been his firstborn.

Oren stirred beside her. "Jarah, I forgot to tell you something about Hannah."

"Yes?"

"After she left Samuel at the tabernacle with the priest,

Adonai gave her seven other children."

Jarah swallowed a lump in her throat. "Isn't that just like our God?"

Chapter 40

Tova marveled at Eliezer's little hands. He had recently discovered they were under his control and enjoyed reaching for things. "The Most High God cares so much for you, son. He's engraved you on his hands, hands that made the stars and hung them in place. He knows all their names, and He knows yours too."

Tova was glad they had met Jarah and Oren in Jerusalem. Even in the short amount of time they spent together, Jarah had taught Tova much about Adonai. And now Jarah and her husband had arrived in Gibeon! Tova looked forward to learning more. Jarah said Oren planned to teach the people every Sabbath morning, beginning soon, and there would be a school for the boys in Gibeon. When he was older, Eliezer would learn even more than she, and would come home and tell her.

A scorched smell interrupted her musings. "Not again," she cried as she moved the pot of lentils from the hot coals. Quickly she worked to scoop the unburned top layer into a separate pot before it absorbed the charred flavor. As she worked, Menachem entered the hut and picked up Eliezer.

"Tova."

"Oh, Menachem. I'm sorry. I was thinking of Jarah and all I learned from her, and now look at your supper. Will I never learn!"

"Tova, it doesn't matter," Menachem replied soberly. "We have something more important to discuss."

At his tone, Tova set aside the utensils and looked at him with fear in her eyes. "You've been talking with the elders?"

"Yes."

Tova squeezed her eyes shut. "And Benjamin will have to divorce Judith?"

"Yes. Many remember her trip to Rabbah earlier in the year, right around the time of the rites to Moloch."

"But she has family there."

"We both know why she chose to go at the new year."

Tova's slumped shoulders conceded his point.

"One of the goatherds also found a high place outside the town. Many of the women have been going that way frequently."

"Maybe they were collecting dung for their cooking fires."

"Some probably were. Praise be to Adonai that Eliezer's been keeping you busy at home so you weren't accused of worshipping at the high place."

Tova's mind snagged on the word *accused*. "Am I being accused of something else?"

Menachem returned Eliezer to the sleeping mat and crossed to Tova, gripping her upper arms and searching her eyes. "It will be all right, matok. But you have to do something for me that will be difficult for you." He paused. "Unfortunately some charges are being made of guilt by association. You have to keep your distance from Judith."

"That's hard in a town this size."

"Our case has not been decided yet, Tova. All the elders tend to believe your worship of Adonai is genuine. There is no evidence against you besides your birth and your friend. We cannot change the one, but you can limit your contact with Judith for a couple moons until she returns to her family. I need you, Tova. Please, please, do this for me... and our son."

"But she's been my friend as long as I can remember, much longer than I've known anyone here, and now she'll need me more than ever!"

"I'm sorry. I don't see any other way."

Tova collapsed against her husband and wept.

Chapter 41

The knocking sound merged into Jarah's dreams until a voice roused her. "Jarah, it's time. Naama needs your help."

Oren opened the door to Gili, who said, "The midwife's busy delivering a baby. I'm going to wait to escort her back to our house. I brought the donkey so she can ride and we can get back as quickly as possible."

Jarah threw on a cloak and shoved her feet into her sandals. Bleary-eyed she grabbed a bundle of soft cloth and a sharpened knife.

As Oren lit the oil lamp, Jarah splashed water on her face. She figured the fourth watch would soon draw to a close with the dawn. *Had Naama been in labor all night?*

The couple set out at a brisk pace from their house in the center of Gibeon to Ariel's vineyard on the outskirts. The sky was lightening as they crested the hill looking down on his property.

When Jarah entered the hut, she asked Ariel to fetch more clean water. "How strong are the pains?" she asked her friend.

"Like being ripped open by a lion. I've been trying not to scream because Ariel's been pacing around and coming back to peer into my face. I'm glad you gave him something to do."

"The first thing Aunt Pazit did at a birth was send the men away. She said it was far easier. Do you want a piece of leather to bite?"

"Not now. Maybe later."

"Has your water broken?"

"No."

"Maybe the midwife will get here in time."

Naama grimaced with the next contraction. "Unhh. My water broke."

As Jarah helped Naama into a dry dress, she noticed dark streaks on the wet robe. She looked for a wet spot on the dirt floor and saw the same dark color.

Naama noticed her friend's scrutiny. "What are you looking at?"

Jarah held up the robe. Naama blanched.

"Do you know what it means?"

"The baby's waste is already in my womb."

Jarah didn't want to ask about the effects on the baby. She had only attended a few births, and in each case the water had broken clear. *Adonai, help. Please hurry the midwife along.*

"I need to have the baby as soon as possible so he doesn't breathe it in. Let's walk."

Jarah took Naama's arm, and the two circled the small room innumerable times, pausing for contractions. Naama's grip on her arm drew blood. Jarah ran through a mental list of the women in Gibeon. Amaris would have been the perfect choice, but she and her family were in Jerusalem, and so far the Gibeonites hadn't been friendly. "Naama, which of the women has a lot of children?"

Naama thought for a moment. "Carmela has quite a few, some grown, and some still young." Her face twisted in pain. "It's hard to think. That's the best I can come up with."

"That's fine. If she's not the right woman, she'll know who is. I'm going to send Oren to see if she'll come." Jarah stepped outside and held a quiet conversation with her husband.

When she returned, Naama was standing in the same place, soaked with perspiration.

"My aunt always checked for the baby's head. Do you want me to try?"

"Yes. Rinse your hands first. My softa said it was safer that way. If the baby's head isn't in the downward position…"

"You told me the midwife said it was. I'm sure he's fine."

Please, Adonai, let this baby be in the right position. I don't know what to do if he's not headfirst. "Yes, there's his head. I think he's coming soon."

"When I need to push, I'll tell you. You have to make sure the cord isn't wrapped around his neck."

"How?"

"You reach in and feel around the base of his head with your fingers."

Jarah wasn't sure how she'd manage. "Do you think it's a boy or a girl?" she asked in order to distract both of them.

"I hope it's a boy, for Ariel's sake. I don't ever want to do this again, though I suppose I will."

"First babies are supposed to be the hardest."

"Yes, well, consider trying to squeeze a grape through the eye of a needle."

Jarah almost laughed at her friend's comparison. "You're not quite like a needle. Think of a bee forcing its way into a closed flower. The petals give."

Naama grunted. "Okay, time to push. I'm going to need that leather now."

Jarah rinsed her hands as Naama squatted, leaning on a stool. As she inserted her hand, Naama pushed her away for a contraction and then said, "Now. Quickly."

Jarah felt carefully around the neck. "I don't feel the cord." *Dear God, please...*

Naama screamed, and Jarah scrambled for the leather, giving it to her friend and positioning herself to catch the baby. "I see hair. Lots of hair. Come on, Naama. You can do it."

At the next push, the head emerged. The baby's face looked more blue than pink. Jarah's heart sped up. *Please, Adonai, Giver of life, breathe life into this baby.*

Another push, and a large son slid into Jarah's hands. Jarah quickly sliced the cord.

"Give him to me," Naama said, sitting on the stool. She put her index finger into the newborn's mouth and swiped around thoroughly, drawing her finger out twice to wipe off a murky stickiness. Then she turned him over on her lap and slapped his bottom gently. When he didn't respond, she repeated her actions with more force.

Jarah held her breath. Naama cleaned out her son's mouth again and swatted him. Jarah could sense her growing frustration. Naama turned him over again and felt for a heartbeat. She began to wail, clutching her firstborn.

Jarah put her arms around her friend. They were both crying, but Jarah needed to finish tending to the afterbirth or Naama could sicken. She was afraid to try to take the babe, so she dragged a bench in front of Naama and told her to lean on it. Uncomprehending, Naama stopped wailing long enough to stare. Jarah gently pushed her into position and pulled on the cord, releasing a flood of blood.

Was that normal? Aunt Pazit always handed me the baby and tended to the new mother herself. Why didn't someone come to help? Adonai, where are You?

Jarah washed the blood from her hands and brought water to Naama who surrendered the baby to be bathed. Jarah first felt for a pulse in his sturdy little arm. Nothing. He looked like a strong baby. *Breathing in waste can kill a healthy baby? So much I don't know.*

Naama was shaking. Jarah used clean cloth to verify the bleeding had slowed and helped Naama to her sleeping pallet. Now she had to face the men. She stumbled out of the hut into an early morning drizzle. Miserably, she gestured to the hut. "I'm so sorry, Ariel. Naama needs you."

Ariel's face crumpled like a little boy's, but he nodded manfully and went to his wife. Jarah collapsed against Oren and cried. "Their baby died."

"I know. So did Ariel. We never heard a child's cry, but we heard you and Naama weeping. Is Naama all right?"

"I don't know. I never took care of a new mother before. Why didn't someone else come?"

"Carmela said she would come as soon as she was able."

"Didn't she know the midwife was at another birth and we

needed her experience?"

"I asked her to come back with me, offering to wait until she was ready, but she said no, one of her children would accompany her."

"What is wrong with these people? They know Naama has no family here. In Babylon, more women came to every birth than were needed. A few would return home and prepare food, so the new mother wouldn't have to think about meals for a couple of days."

Jarah leaned back and swiped at her face. As she did, she saw movement among the vines. Tova stepped into the small clearing around the limestone cottage. She was lugging a child and a pot covered with flat bread. When she saw Jarah's face, she stopped dead and carefully set the pot down. "Naama's baby?" she faltered.

Jarah's lip curled downward. She couldn't speak without more tears.

"The babe died," Oren said.

"Oh, no!" the young woman clutched her child closer, gazing into his face. "She saved Eliezer. He wasn't breathing, but she cleaned out his mouth and made him breathe. He would have died if it hadn't been for her!"

"The midwife didn't attend you either?" Oren asked.

"No, she had a fever. Carmela would have come, but her children were sick too, so Naama told her to stay home. I can't believe this happened to her.

"Adonai, where are you?" she asked, lifting her face to the sky. "Naama was so good to me, so good. Why take her child?" Tova turned her attention back to the couple. "You taught me so much in Jerusalem. Do you know why?"

Jarah moved forward to embrace Tova and peek at Eliezer, who lay sleeping against his mother's chest. "I don't have any answers. All I know is Adonai's ways are not ours. And Naama will need all the friends she can get these next few days."

"I brought food. I'll bring more tomorrow."

"How did you know Naama's baby was coming?"

"I made Judith promise to tell me. She and her family live in the vineyard house nearer town. She doesn't like Tova's family because of their claiming her vineyard, but she saw what Naama did for me at Eliezer's birth. She said she'd tell me when Naama's time came. I'd hoped to help with the birth, but she just came by a little while ago. I hurried to nurse Eliezer and gather food. I couldn't walk fast with this load."

"I'm glad you came. Why didn't more women come?"

"Naama's an outsider whose family laid claim to Benjamin and Judith's vineyard. Judith's an Ammonite, so the women don't care much about her, but Benjamin's one of their own. All his family live here, except for one brother, so they took up his cause and exclude Naama."

"But you're helping Naama because she helped you?"

"I tried to be friendly from the beginning. I know how she feels," Tova answered.

"So the women don't accept you either?"

"I've never been fully embraced by the people here, but since Ezra's divorce decree, the women have been more suspicious of me. I know I'm being scrutinized. They watch to see if I'll go to an altar to Moloch outside of town. I never have."

Tova straightened with resolve. "I serve the One True God, and I'm not hiding anything. What bothers me is having to stay away from Judith, so I'm not divorced like she will be. She needs a friend right now, and she's miffed at me for keeping away from her. Menachem told me I must, for his sake and Eliezer's, not just mine. That's probably why she took her sweet time telling me about Naama."

Chapter 42

A young Jew with a familiar face stood at the wooden door in front of their chambers. Hadassah tried to place him. Was he one of the Levites?

"Shalom. I bring news from your sister," the lad began.

"Which sister?" Hadassah asked nervously.

"Miriam, wife of my cousin Samuel. I'm David."

Hadassah decided she had seen him at the wedding. "Come in. Would you like some water?"

"Yes, thank you. Your sister and her husband send greetings."

Hadassah smiled. "How are they?"

"Not to alarm you, but my cousin requests your presence. Miriam broke her ankle, and although Samuel's family can easily help them, Samuel feels that Miriam needs you."

Hadassah winced. "Is she in pain? How long ago did she break it?"

"I don't know about the pain. She's been staying indoors. The accident happened a few days ago. Since my father and I were coming to Jerusalem to sell wine, Samuel asked me to speak with you. We return tomorrow or the next day if you'd like to ride in our donkey cart with us. My sister who's of marrying age came too, so you could travel with us. It will take all day, but we'll reach Gibeon before nightfall."

Hadassah sank down on a stool. "I need to talk with my father, but I'd like to go. How can I reach you? Better yet, would your sister like to stay here with us while your family's in Jerusalem?"

"I'm sure she'd appreciate your hospitality. Better than sleeping on the ground near our cart. I'll bring her after our work in the marketplace is done this afternoon."

"Excellent. I'll try to talk with my father before then."

"My father says he knows your father is very important and has many matters to attend to, so if you can't speak with him before this evening, we'll wait as necessary."

Surprised at their perception of her father, all Hadassah could manage was "Thank you, David."

∞∞∞

"Of course you must go, child. Adin and I will manage," Ezra said when she found him before the evening sacrifice. He had been teaching Moses' words from the second law to a few young priests whom he dismissed when she waved at him from the women's courtyard.

"I'll let them know I can leave at dawn."

∞∞∞

Leaving as soon as light began to touch the city, the foursome reached Gibeon in late afternoon. David guided Hadassah to her sister's limestone home, which was squeezed between two larger domiciles. She embraced Miriam carefully. Before she could remove her sandals and wash her dusty feet, Amaris bustled in. "Shalom, Hadassah. Rest and catch up with your sister after your journey. I'll send my daughters to draw and deliver the evening water."

Hadassah hugged Amaris. "That's very thoughtful. But one day in a donkey cart hardly compares to walking five moons from Susa to Jerusalem." The women laughed.

"It's a good thing this didn't happen then," Miriam said, gesturing to her foot.

"It's a miracle it didn't when you climbed the ziggurat in Ur," Hadassah scolded.

"Or when Rebekah and I climbed the Jerusalem ruins," Miriam added.

Amaris threw her arms into the air, "So this will be a regular occurrence?"

"No, no, esteemed mother-of-my-husband."

Amaris squeezed Miriam's hand and then rose and turned to Hadassah. "Come eat with us tonight."

Hadassah looked at Miriam lying on a pallet, foot propped up on a blanket. Amaris followed her gaze. "Samuel carries her over for the evening meal. She shouldn't put any weight on her leg."

Hadassah nodded and crouched near her sister's foot. "May I?"

"Yes."

Hadassah unwrapped a long strip of linen cloth to view the black and blue joint. "Is it painful?"

"It aches. Amaris brews tea to help me sleep at night."

"How'd you manage this?"

"I was gathering dried animal dung in the fields and sank into an animal's hole. I heard it crack."

Hadassah surveyed her sister intently. "Out with the entire story, little sister."

"That is the story." Miriam feigned innocence.

"You didn't simply step into a hole, did you?"

"We—ll…I was moving faster than the tortoise's crawl you call a walk."

"Were you running?"

"Yes, but only because someone was chasing me."

"Chasing you!"

"Ummm. Yes."

"Who was chasing you? Isn't it safe here?"

"It's perfectly safe." Miriam huffed. "Samuel's youngest brother was after me."

"Isn't he seven?"

"Turned eight with the last moon."

"Why was he after you?" Hadassah demanded.

"We were racing."

"Of course you were," Hadassah said, shaking her head. "Miriam, you're a married woman now. You can't race little boys."

"No one would know about it if I hadn't broken my ankle. And he says I'm his favorite aunt."

"I believe the second statement. I'm not so sure about the first," Hadassah sighed. "What's done is done. Let me dampen this bandage to keep the swelling down."

Chapter 43

After a restless night due to new surroundings, Hadassah rose early to fill the water pots from the spring in Gibeon. As she walked through the center of the town, she admired the homes. She glimpsed full-grown trees in their courtyards and vines climbing front walls.

Steep spiraling steps descended to the pool, and the rock walls caused conversations to carry. As Hadassah scooped water from a pool formed by the spring, she listened to the chatter.

"If she dies, it will serve them right," a matron declared.

"Imagine them trying to take Benjamin's vineyard when he's living on it with his family," a young woman answered.

"We're not safe in our own homes," another clucked.

"I'm glad my husband's family has lived here since King Saul's time. No one will try to dispute our right to our land," the young woman replied. "How long has your family been here, Carmela?"

"Don't rightly know. Since Joshua divided the land, I think," the matron answered.

"I'd stick with that if any more Jews come back from Persia and Babylon."

"Don't you worry."

The trio moved up the stairs out of Hadassah's hearing. *Is this how we're viewed in the villages? In Jerusalem, the merchants welcomed the increased business. Not all the priests were happy about sharing their power, but the returning priests took on a great deal of work which defused most of the tension, except the trouble with Joiada and his brothers. Whom were the women discussing?* Jarah and Naama had settled in Gibeon. Was one of them in trouble?

Lugging her jar up the steps, Hadassah rushed back to the house and quickly mixed bread dough. She set it to rise on the hearth and stoked the coals, adding a few branches. "Miriam, I know I just got here, but I need to go check on Jarah."

"Go. I usually nap in the mornings to make up for the sleep I lose at night." Miriam gave directions to Jarah's home.

Hadassah found the house without trouble. It was closer to the city center than Miriam's, and ample in size, even for the family Jarah and Oren wanted. The white limestone shone in the morning sunlight. Jarah had already added a white coat to brighten up the previously abandoned home.

"Hadassah!" Jarah spied her through the open door. "The face of a friend is one of God's best gifts." Jarah enfolded her in a hug and drew her inside. "I've missed you."

"I've missed you too. Miriam broke her ankle, so Samuel sent for me."

"Is she trying to get around?"

"No, not yet. There's still a lot of pain, especially at night. But I'm sure as soon as she's feeling better, she'll want to be up and around."

"And your job is to keep her down?"

"Something like that."

"Samuel's smarter than I gave him credit for. Already knows his bride's stubborn as a donkey."

Hadassah laughed. "So far it's been easy, but you're right, it's going to get tougher. I'm glad to find you looking well."

"I'm great. Look at this house, Hadassah, and it's all ours. I was a little girl the last time I had a home where I really belonged."

Hadassah reveled in the pleasure reflected on her friend's face. Then she remembered the conversation she had overheard at Gibeon's pool. "Jarah, is Naama well? Has the baby arrived?"

Jarah sank onto a stool and covered her face with her hands. "No, and yes, her son arrived but he didn't..." Jarah stopped, overcome.

"Is Naama..."

"She's alive, but it's like something inside her died. She lost

167

the will to live, along with a lot of blood. I'm going to see her as soon as I finish up here. I don't think she should be alone. Ariel or Gili is usually there, but they don't know what to do for her. Neither do I, but I go and talk to her, help her with the cooking."

"Miriam said she would nap this morning. You take care of your house and get your work done this morning. I'll go now and won't leave until you come. That way she'll have company most of the day."

"I'm glad you're here."

"Me too. Evidently Adonai brought me at just the right time."

Hadassah followed Jarah's directions along the main street of Gibeon with its neat white homes. Leaving the town, she followed a little-traveled ribbon of white dust that divided the terraces clinging to rocky hillsides. The grape vines were dormant, but she imagined them heavy with grapes, row after row. She only glimpsed two limestone cottages before reaching a bend in the road that climbed up a small hill.

Hadassah left the footpath and walked between rows of brown vines. Some vines had been pruned recently, tender inner flesh exposed where a knife had lopped off a branch. Rounding a curve on the terraced hill, Hadassah caught her breath when she spied a man walking with a loose, long-legged gait toward her. The vinedresser walked like Jedidiah! Jedidiah had been tall, and as Hadassah neared, she saw that the olive-skinned man also towered above her. He bent to a vine, but straightened as she approached.

She lifted a hand in greeting, "Shalom. I'm searching for the home of my friend Naama." Hadassah chose not to use Ariel's name, knowing this man must have owned the entire vineyard before Ariel claimed part of it.

He gestured behind him. "Keep walking, past the first cottage, to the end of the vineyard. Her home lies beyond the vines." His face was serious, but Hadassah thought his deep brown eyes seemed kind. "I hope you can help her."

Her pulse quickened. "Thank you."

Hadassah easily located the cottage. No life stirred until she called a greeting outside the door. The door scraped inward over the dirt floor to reveal Naama, pale, with dark hair hanging in tangles. Her face brightened briefly at the sight of her friend before it crumpled. She collapsed in Hadassah's arms and sobbed.

Hadassah stroked her hair, gently working out some of the tangles, as Naama cried until her face was red and splotchy. Hadassah sank onto a bench near the door, and Naama slumped at her feet, with her head in Hadassah's lap.

"God's punishing me," Naama whispered. "Adonai knew I didn't want my baby at first, but that was just at the beginning. He was a big, strong boy. Ariel would have been so proud of him. We were going to name him Otanes, for my father." Tears slipped silently down her face.

Hadassah shook her head. "No, no, Naama. The Almighty doesn't work like that. He created you and your baby. I'm sorry about the little fellow, but Adonai understood how you felt at the beginning and the reasons you felt that way. And He saw how your love for the child grew as Otanes grew in your womb."

"God knows all that?"

"Absolutely. He knows everything."

Naama looked more scared than comforted, so Hadassah continued, "God is good and merciful."

"Then why couldn't he let Otanes live?"

"I don't know." The women were quiet for long moments, listening to the sighing of the wind. "Losing children seems to be a woman's lot in life. Do you know any woman who hasn't lost a pregnancy, baby, or child?"

Naama considered the question. "No, my softa used to say one out of every three babies doesn't make it to adulthood. She saw a lot of babies die."

"What would she tell you now?"

"The baby was well-formed. He just wasn't born soon enough," Naama's voice caught. "She'd also say this problem wasn't likely to happen again."

"There! We'll start praying for a healthy child for you and

Ariel."

"She would tell me not to try for another child too soon."

"Wise advice."

"But there are scores of other things that can go wrong with a pregnancy or birth," Naama worried.

"We'll pray those away. Did you know I once had a little brother?"

"No, I thought you only had sisters."

"Adin was a twin at birth. Joel lived about a year, but he was never healthy. He had difficulty breathing. I remember my em crying for him but saying he was better off in Paradise."

"And then your em died too?" Naama asked softly.

"She lived for a year or so. She wasn't strong after the twins' birth. They came too early. After my em died, the Queen told me she was in Paradise looking after Joel."

"That's a comfort. I can picture a big, strong man cradling his grandson."

"Your father? Yes, the queen spoke of him being in Paradise, too."

A look of peace settled across Naama's face. "I need to hold onto that picture—my abba holding his namesake."

∞∞∞

"Tova, could you watch Hen for me while I look for fuel to start my fire? I'm almost out. I'd be able to carry more."

Tova slowly rose and approached her childhood friend.

"Don't worry. I ducked in while no one's out in the street. I'll be careful when I leave too."

"Oh, Judith! I can't. Didn't Benjamin tell you?"

"Tell me what? He hasn't been around much. I've been cowering inside for a week, and now I need fuel for my fire. Won't you help me?"

"I can't, Judith. I promised Menachem. The elders haven't decided our case yet, so he thinks it will be better if I don't associate with you right now. I want to stay here, Judith. In Yehud, where Moloch's not worshipped. I don't want to go back to my old life."

"I'm not going back to *my* old life either. Remember all the suitors I had? Who will want me now, especially since I have a half-Jewish baby girl?" Judith's dark eyes smoldered. "Fine! I'll stay away from you. Forget I ever asked." She flounced out the front door.

Menachem entered as soon as she left. "Tova, why were you speaking with her? Most of the village will know she's been here."

Tova couldn't answer. She was crying too hard.

∞∞∞

"Would Adonai really have me turn my back on a friend?" Tova asked Menachem later that night as they lay on their sleeping mats.

Menachem sighed. "As a general rule, I'd say no, Tova, but these are bad times. Hundreds of men are divorcing their wives and sending away their children. I didn't think Adonai favored divorce, but in this case there's something more elemental at stake."

"How can there be anything more basic than the family, beginning with a man and his wife?"

"Oren said obedience to the Most High is more important than anything, including family. Please, matok, at this point you're only losing a good friend. Do you want to lose me?"

"No, of course not," Tova assured him. *But even more, I don't want to lose the opportunity to live in this land where Adonai is worshipped and Moloch isn't. I'll have to avoid Judith like Menachem says and trust Adonai for the rest.*

Chapter 44

Hadassah traveled back to Jerusalem with the elders from Gibeon and the men who were divorcing their wives. It was the Gibeonites' turn to appear before the priests. She felt sorry for the men who plodded along, heads down with the weight of their dying families on their shoulders. She recognized the man who had helped her find Naama's home, and her heart ached.

What will happen to their wives when they return to the places of their birth? This will stir up a political storm that will affect us all for years to come, not to mention the cost to these families. I know their pain. On days like today I want to lie down and die from the anguish. It's almost as bad as right after Jedidiah's death.

As soon as she greeted Adin, she began preparing lentils to accompany the meat their father would bring from the sacrifices. After Ezra arrived bearing a haunch of lamb, the small family sat to eat. Hadassah spoke of Miriam and Samuel and Amaris' family, but she noticed her father seemed distant. Finally he said, "You'll need to remarry, Little Star."

Hadassah stared at her father wide-eyed. "Why?" she choked.

"You've seen the men who come day after day to divorce their wives. They'll need new wives."

She jumped up from her stool at the table and rushed out into the night.

Ezra looked after her in puzzlement.

Adin cleared her throat. "Have you forgotten what day it is, abba?"

When her father stared at her blankly, Adin continued softly,

"It's been thirteen moons since Jedidiah died."

Ezra wished the ground would open and swallow him. He looked distractedly at the door through which Hadassah had escaped.

"I didn't mark the anniversaries of your mother's death, mostly because I lived in a haze. She was never strong after birthing you twins and took it hard when your brother Joel died in the battle of Purim. She held on for nearly two years, but she was fading the entire time, and finally my spunky, vibrant Rachel didn't wake up one morning." Ezra kneaded his eyes with his hands.

Adin rose and draped her arm around him.

"I didn't notice the passage of time, until the day you turned five and I woke up and realized the last three years had disappeared. You, Miriam, and Rebekah were running wild, in rags. Our house was falling down around us. It's a mercy none of you were hurt playing in the mess. Our pottery, what little was left from the set I made your mother for our wedding, was chipped or cracked."

"Where was Hadassah? She's always been good at looking after things."

"She had already begun serving the queen. Esther must have questioned what kind of father I was since I failed to visit or send for Hadassah. But that day the Almighty smote my heart. I fashioned new pottery at my family's shop and gave a piece to each of you after it was kilned."

"I remember. Mine had a rose on it!"

"Yes, I spent extra time on yours as your birthday gift."

"It's a shame Miriam and Rebekah were clumsy with breakables," Adin lamented. "I loved my plate."

Ezra chuckled. "They were the most rambunctious children on the street. Even the boys couldn't match their destructive behavior. I'm sorry they broke your plate." He squeezed his daughter's arm. "Do you remember the day I bought you new robes and we all went to the palace to visit Hadassah? Esther spent a long time talking with me. She loved your mother almost as much as I did. I'm sorry she didn't ever share the kind of love your mother and I had. Your mother and I were blessed of Adonai." He sighed, "I just wish it had lasted longer."

"Love never dies, Abba. Em is still alive."

"How did you become so wise?"

Adin ignored his question. "You know *you* could marry again."

"I know, but I've never wanted to, so I should be more sensitive to how Hadassah feels. The difference is that I have you girls. I want Hadassah to know the joy of children."

"So do I, but we can't force her. She needs to find her own joy, whether she remarries or not."

∞∞∞

Ezra's beautiful daughter stumbled by Ctesias. Garbed as a Jew, he had sneaked into the courtyard and been studying the Jews' temple to plan his raid. He hid in the shadows of the nearest wall, but she was too preoccupied to notice him.

Ctesias' mind raced with the possibilities. A few Jewish men were saying prayers nearby, so he needed to wait. He fingered his dagger as he considered killing her. A murder in the temple would make an impression on these miserable Jews, but killing one woman hardly avenged his father's death and his family's disgrace.

He should grab her and keep her hidden until after his band raided the temple and left Jerusalem. They could deal with her in the desert on their return trip. Plus the men could get a little pleasure out of her first. They were getting restless. No one had expected this business to take them so far from home and consume so much time.

As the Jews faded one by one into the darkness after finishing their prayers, the woman continued to cry, completely unaware of his presence. Just as the last one disappeared through the gate, Ctesias heard whistling.

A brawny Levite strode through the gate with arms full of wood. After dropping the wood beside a bronze altar, he wiped sweat from his forehead and cocked his head, listening. Following the sound of weeping, he approached the woman. "Are you all right?"

Ctesias couldn't hear her reply.

"You can't stay out here at this time of night. It's not safe."

Although the man outweighed him, Ctesias figured he could win a fight with a surprise attack. He would go for the Jew's throat. Even if he missed and hit his face or chest, he should be able to grab the girl and get away.

∞∞∞

When Hadassah didn't return during the first watch, Ezra became worried and started searching for her. She was huddled against one of the temple walls speaking in a thick, tear-soaked voice with one of the Levites, "I hadn't noticed how late it had gotten. There were others praying when I came. I'll return to my chamber now."

The Levite caught sight of Ezra. "Here's your father to take you safely home." He moved farther away to give them privacy.

Ezra saw him scan the area, peering into the shadows beyond the torches.

Ezra turned his full attention to his daughter. "I'm sorry, Hadassah. I didn't realize what day it is. Adin reminded me. I know you're not ready yet, and I'm sorry for my thoughtless words."

His daughter sniffed, and he put an arm around her as they returned to their chamber.

"Even though these men made wrong choices, I feel sorry for them. There was a handsome young fellow today from the city of Gibeon. His wife just had a baby, and he swears she serves the Most High. But the town's elders disagree. They strongly suspect her of helping to rebuild a high place outside the city. He's broken-hearted. Now he must return home and send them both away. Most of the men acknowledge their wives' idolatry and the necessity of the divorces, but this man... I hope we made the right decision."

Ctesias felt like cursing but remained hidden, barely breathing as the Levite examined the area again and exited the temple courtyard.

Chapter 45

Oren looked up from his roasted grain as Jarah burst through the door. She was white and shaking. He dropped the grain and grabbed her hands. "Are you hurt? What's wrong?" he asked, studying her for any sign of injury.

She sank onto a bench, and he sat with her. "I...I know why Carmela didn't come when Naama's baby was born. At least I think I do."

"Why?"

"She's married to Benjamin's eldest brother. I was talking to her married daughter at the spring, and she mentioned her uncle Benjamin. Oren, do you think she refused to help at a birth because of some *vines*?"

"She said one of the children became violently ill, but they all looked fine to me when I talked to her and her husband."

"How could this happen? How could she refuse to help Naama? The baby *died*! I didn't know what to do for him." Jarah started to cry.

"It's wicked to ignore your neighbor's need, but the outcome would have been the same in this case. Naama knew what to do, and she tried, but the baby was born too late. Carmela's presence wouldn't have changed the end result."

Jarah wiped her face on her sleeve, her usually jovial face twisted with disgust. "So it's not murder, but we could have needed her help. Ay! We're supposed to live among God's people now, but my Persian neighbors were better than this."

Yehud isn't all we hoped it would be. Oren hugged his wife. Her sobs had quieted to hiccups when she broke into fresh tears.

"And now the gossip at the spring is that Naama should be divorced because she's a pagan too."

"Why do the townspeople think she's heathen?"

"When they buried the baby, Naama named her son Otanes after her deceased father. It's a Persian name."

"I didn't know that."

"I told you on the journey out here. She makes no secret of it. Her mother converted when Mordecai came to power as the king's advisor and many people became Jews."

"Then her family have been proselytes for two generations. She's completely safe. The Gibeonites are just trying to cause trouble for her, probably because of the vineyard. I didn't hear any discussion among the elders about Ariel and Naama. The elders and men who will be issued divorces already left for Jerusalem. They should return home tomorrow or the next day. I know Ariel didn't go.

"Don't fret. The elders decided that Judith, the Ammonitess whose family owned the vineyard, should be divorced. Her husband vowed to dispute their decision before the priests and Ezra himself. I don't think he'll succeed, and the land won't be returned to her even though it was her dowry. I wouldn't be surprised if the whole vineyard were returned to Ariel and his family."

∞∞∞

Benjamin walked so slowly the others began nagging him to hurry. He felt like he was trying to drag Mt. Zion along with him. *How can I face Judith? How can I send her and Hen away? They're woven into the fabric of my soul. None of us will survive. Judith will need to remarry.* The image of his wife with another man made him stop and heave into the bushes.

Chapter 46

When High Priest Eliashib called a meeting of all priests, Joiada arrived with an entourage of young men, including his brother Eli. Eliashib was seated while David hovered behind his father's huge chair. Other priests stood or sat on stools. Joiada leaned against a wall, positioning himself where he could view both Ezra and his father.

As soon as Joiada's group settled into their places, Eliashib called the gathering to order and offered a prayer for wisdom. "Ezra has already outlined his plan to our council. Most of you have heard of the idea of the bet 'amma by now. You can ask questions before we reach a consensus." He nodded to Ezra.

"Brothers, thank you for your willingness to follow God's law and officiate the divorces. Now that these painful proceedings are complete, let's establish a bet 'amma in each city and village so the people will know God's law. Many of our men were ignorant of God's command to marry only daughters of Israel."

"Won't the people stop coming to temple if they have a place of worship in their own cities?" a young priest asked.

"The bet 'amma would be for instruction on the Sabbath, not for Passover, the Feast of Tabernacles, or Yom Kippur," Ezra replied.

"What about towns close to Jerusalem?"

"Anyone close by would come to worship at the temple."

"Would every tiny community have one?" a gray-bearded priest inquired.

"During our captivity, we established one bet 'amma for every ten Jewish men. This number seemed to work well."

"Who will teach in the bet 'amma?" an adolescent questioned.

"The priests and Levites who aren't fulfilling their temple service."

"But will we have enough for all our towns? Many villages won't have a qualified leader since we live in the cities of the Levites."

"Now that we have many new priests, we could set up a rotation of service to God which includes temple service and bet 'amma service," Ezra said.

Whispering broke out among the priests. Joiada surmised they were as alarmed by this idea as he was. *I don't want to be sent to some tiny backwater of a community. I want to stay here, in the seat of power.*

"It's worthy of consideration," the old priest declared.

"Won't the teaching differ from place to place since there will be so many teachers?" Joiada asked. "Perhaps Ezra should go from village to village in order to maintain consistency."

"It's too vast a job for one man," Eliashib said thoughtfully.

"I would gladly help set up bet 'ammas, but they need to grow into self-sustaining communities guided by the Torah, writings, and prophecies," Ezra added.

"It would be better for Ezra to train the leaders," the elderly priest said.

"I agree." Eliashib nodded.

"Every Sabbath on our journey here I taught the men. Many asked questions and learned a great deal in those five moons. Of course, walking that far provides ample time for meditation," Ezra added with a smile. His face took on its usual serious mien. "Although not all are sons of Levi, some of these men are ready and willing to teach. They are accustomed to these places of worship and could establish them according to the pattern begun by our prophet Ezekiel."

"What type of pattern?"

"Three men read portions of the Torah. The last delivers a message based on the reading."

"We'd need many copies of the holy books so each bet 'amma

has its own set," a scrawny priest said.

"There are only five scribes working in our scroll room," Eli said.

"Can you hire more, Eli?" Eliashib asked.

"Yes, I'll see to it this afternoon."

"Do the people worship or simply listen to teaching?" the leader of the singing Levites asked.

"The time begins with prayer and ends with singing David's songs," Ezra assured him.

"It is good," the leader said.

"Are we agreed to establish bet 'ammas, fellow priests?" Eliashib asked, searching the room for signs of assent.

Most of the priests nodded in agreement. A few stood silently, like Joiada.

I'm not sure I like this. I'm not sure I like this at all.

The next morning Benjamin and one of the elders of Gibeon came to Judith's little white house with the *Get*. It dissolved their marriage. Judith was to have no further contact with Benjamin. Tomorrow all the Ammonite women would be gathered and escorted by a merchant caravan traveling through Gibeon to Rabbah.

After rousing herself from the devastating news, Judith began to prepare for the journey. She stuffed her two favorite robes into a leather bag. She added her kohl and a carefully sealed jar of persimmon perfume. She would have to make more skin balm when she reached Rabbah. The large pot wouldn't fit. How would she be able to carry these few necessities, food, water, and Hen? She spent a long, lonely day and was settling down to cry herself to sleep when Tova silently appeared.

"I came the long way so no one would see," she whispered. "I'm so sorry, Judith. Benjamin came and spoke to me. He wants you to take the coins hidden in the red jar. He'll send more to replace your dowry as soon as he can. He's beside himself, Judith. He wanted to hold Hen again and say good-bye, but the elders have watched him all day."

"I know," Judith said dully. "I could see it in his eyes this morning."

"Shalom, Judith," Tova said as she hugged her.

Judith laughed mirthlessly. "There is no peace for me. I'll tell your family you're still married, but won't be coming to see them. Good-bye, Tova."

Chapter 47

Hadassah wanted to purchase good cloth for a new robe for Adin. As they sewed the priestly garments, Hadassah had seen Adin finger the colorful cloth, and she had finally noticed the threadbare state of Adin's three dresses. She had darics the queen had given her before she departed from Susa, so she would be able to buy material at the market.

She was disappointed the wares did not compare to those available in Persia, but what could she expect? Susa was one of the capitals of a great empire. Jerusalem, the city of the Most High, had barely survived. Its walls lay in ruins still.

This silk was inferior, but Adin would appreciate the turquoise color, and it was the best she could find in the entire *souk*. If she left immediately, she could walk back to the temple the long way, following the wall, and still arrive home in time to prepare the evening meal. Next time Oren came to fulfill his priestly rotation she would send thread to Jarah, requesting a fine piece of linen. Adin would gain two new sets of clothes.

Ctesias couldn't believe his good luck when he spied the woman leaving the marketplace toward the ruined walls. The dirt path beside the wall might be deserted. This could be his chance! Tomorrow night there would be no moon, and his men would rob the temple. Today he could exact revenge on the Jews' leader.

He wheeled his mount, scattering gravel and an old woman's pomegranates. After positioning two Bactrians between Ezra's daughter and the market, he dashed up a street that would intersect the path beside the wall.

Hadassah ambled along, humming "The Lord has done great things for us, and we are filled with joy." *The Most High delivered me from life in the harem. He hasn't forgotten me. Just like Jarah said, I'm written on the palms of his hands. But how can he care for so many of us at the same time?*

Deep in meditation, Hadassah looked up when a shadow blocked the sun. A man mounted on an Arabian stallion had stopped in the pathway. She hesitated. He seemed menacing.

When he commanded her to halt, she started back the way she had come, but spied two men lounging by the path, possibly blocking her escape. She could tell they were Bactrians by their dress--baggy trousers underneath belted tunics.

Are they innocent passerby or in league with the rider? It's not going to matter because I won't make it far before the rider catches up.

Hitching up her long skirts so she could flee without tripping, Hadassah scrambled up the broken walls. Her headdress slipped down over her eyes, so she snatched it off.

The rider galloped to the wall and threw himself off his mount, scrambling after her.

When Hadassah saw the Bactrians climb the wall, she realized they were working with the Persian. She had almost reached the rock where Miriam had faltered. If she could reach it, perhaps she could use her knowledge of its balance in her favor. She kept looking to the road, desperate for aid, but no one passed by. *Please, Adonai. Please help me.*

"You have lovely ankles, beautiful girl," the man behind her mocked. "And that silky hair. I can't wait to…"

Hadassah threw her headdress in his face and leaped to the precariously positioned rock. Ctesias, temporarily blinded, slowed to a walk, sure of his quarry, but the other two approached swiftly toward the unsupported ledge of stone. Hadassah gathered herself for her next jump, knowing it must be timed perfectly. As the first stepped onto the other end of the long slab, she bounded to the next rock, the one Rebekah had stood on as she guided Miriam to safety.

Then she sprinted over the rubble and outside the city. She heard two men yelling and the crash of falling rock over the sound of her ragged breathing.

Ctesias looked in disbelief at the mangled form of his best scout, torso crushed. By the time he freed the other's leg, Hadassah was nowhere to be seen. The leg was merely bruised, not broken, and the two hobbled back to Jaspar. Ctesias allowed the invalid to ride, so they could get away more quickly. The noise alone should attract a crowd. The Jews had little fight in them, but they seemed favored by their god, and his men were outnumbered. So they retreated swiftly to their camp outside town, and the men tended their injured comrade.

∞∞∞∞

Late that night, his Bactrian lieutenant approached him as he sat brooding in the darkness at the edge of camp. "We need to return to our tribe. We're finished with this mission."

Ctesias nodded slowly. Spies had reported increased guards at the temple. He wouldn't get his hands on its gold and silver. They needed to get out before more men died. "We leave at first light. Did you retrieve the body?"

"Five of us went back, but the wall was crawling with Jews. I left two to watch, but if we can't get him before dawn, we'll leave him. We need to pull out of here."

"Agreed."

Ezra lifted a torch and examined what he could see of the body below him. He was thankful his eldest daughter was safe, but what a horrible way for her pursuer to die! There was no way to extricate him. Scavengers would have to do their job.

Ten Levites remained at the wall, looking for Hadassah's

other attackers. Soon the whole city would hear of the incident. The men would carefully guard their wives and daughters.

May this be the end of the problem, Adonai! I thought we would be safe when we reached our land, but our enemies are everywhere. Could they have followed us from Persia? Surely not! We lived there for years, and Hadassah was never bothered. No, they must be passing through Jerusalem. Hadassah is exquisite, and she caught their attention. Surely that was it. They'll move on now.

Chapter 48

Benjamin wandered outside his older brothers' homes, unable to settle down to sleep. His brothers had kept him company until the second watch, trying to keep him from making a decision they believed he would regret. They had finally retired, but Benjamin was pacing like a lion.

Judith is leaving in the morning—forever. I'll never hold her again. She'll never smile at me. I won't see Hen grow up. Will an Ammonite stepfather be kind to her, or will he abuse my precious daughter?

Maybe he should leave Yehud tomorrow and go with Judith. He could raise goats or pick fruit or ask Dael for work.

I had the opportunity to live in Rabah, and I made the choice years ago--I'm a son of Israel. But how could Adonai force me to choose between my family and my God? Adonai created family! And yet, I failed Adonai when I chose to marry outside of my people. I didn't know it was forbidden. The priests didn't read that portion of the writings when I went to temple at Passover. They read about deliverance from Egypt.

Benjamin buried his face in his hands and sobbed.

Does Adonai really expect me to forsake my dependents for a law I never heard before this year's meeting at the temple? I'd already been married for several years, and Hen was conceived before I knew of this sin. Maybe Adonai won't hold me responsible due to circumstances. After all, the priests weren't doing their job.

But that's the reason Ezra came—to teach the people the law of the Most High. And he has to start somewhere, but why does this have to dissolve my family?

He thought again of Judith's beauty and warmth at night. *How will Judith be able to carry Hen and her belongings all the way back to Rabbah? She'll need help. I should pack a few staples on our donkey and return her safely to her family.*

The elders won't like it and might even give the vineyard to Ariel while I'm gone, but so be it. I'll return after Judith and Hen are safe with her family. I'll join the caravan after it leaves Gibeon so no one can stop me.

After gathering the necessities and rolling them in an extra robe, Benjamin lay on his mat for a few hours of sleep before the journey.

As the night wore on, Judith's despair turned to fury—at this leader Ezra who had stirred up a hornet's nest, at Gibeon's elders, at Benjamin, and even at Hen. She tried to picture her future.

What will I do when I return to my father's tents, disgraced and with a baby girl? I might be beaten, though this divorce isn't my fault. Not at all! I've been a good wife, preparing food, picking the harvest, attending to all my husband's needs. He won't find a wife my equal, especially in pleasing his body. I learned well during the festivals. He's wrong to divorce me like this! Over what—a god? I do worship his god. I just choose to worship Moloch too.

Judith's fury turned to a white-hot hatred. *I'll leave Benjamin a message, one he'll never forget.*

∞∞∞∞

Judith stumbled on her way to the high place outside Gibeon, her baby girl slung against her side, thoughts churning like a river in flood. *If only Hen had been a boy! The baby could have been circumcised, and adherence to the law would have helped my case. Now we're being sent away.* She gasped for air as she reached the top of the hill. *I need to hurry so I can leave with the caravan.*

Placing a wide-eyed Hen on the crude altar she and several other women had formed of stone, she removed a sharp knife from its sheath. Usually sacrifices to Moloch were burned alive, but she didn't have time. Plus the cries would alert the villagers. She wanted to be far away from the city before Hen was discovered. Moloch would understand. He had given her a baby daughter, and she was giving Hen back and asking for a good future.

∞∞∞

Tova squinted into the semi-darkness beyond the well. Judith was striding up a hill in the opposite direction from the caravan. An altar of stone sat at the crest of the next hill. The elders were going to destroy it today.

Sensing trouble, Tova abandoned her water jug and followed. When she had almost reached the hilltop, she heard Hen shriek, but the sound was quickly cut off. She saw a flame and smelled a terrible odor. She recognized it from the rites to Moloch she'd witnessed as a child.

Running toward the flames, she glimpsed Judith escaping down the other side of the rise. She wanted to chase her down and shake her, but, carrying Eliezer, she would never catch her. Instead she focused on the figure in the flames. The child was already dead. Judith had thrust a knife into her daughter's heart.

Pierced by Judith's depravity, Tova sank to her knees and sobbed. Her son began wailing with her. Knowing they must not be discovered at the high place, she quieted him and crept back toward Gibeon in the growing light. She still needed to draw water, but first she would find Menachem.

∞∞∞

Benjamin slept longer than he intended but rose purposefully as dawn broke. His last task was to fill a couple of skins with water and disappear into the vineyards until he could leave Gibeon undetected.

Before he could reach the spring and get the water, Tova found him. "Praise to Adonai," she cried, clinging to his arm. "Oh, Benjamin, Menachem and I have been searching for you. You have to come with me."

Benjamin pushed her arm away, stunned by her behavior. No woman touched a man who was not her husband. What could have upset her this much?

Panic rushed in. "Is Judith okay?"

Tova was sobbing now, but shook her head yes. "It's...it's... Hen." She motioned for him to follow her. On their way out of the town, Menachem met them and handed Eliezer to his wife. He told her to return home and lie down.

Benjamin's heart flooded with dread. "What is it?"

"Tova found something terrible. We need to go look for ourselves."

The men walked in silence. There was an acrid smell as they climbed the next hill. Benjamin sniffed the horrible charred odor.

The color drained from Menachem's face. "Tova was right. It's a human sacrifice. Maybe I should go ahead."

Realization hit Benjamin like a bull. As soon as he could breathe, he started to run. Menachem kept pace. As they crested the hill, they saw the slight form smoldering on the altar. Menachem doused it with water from a clay jar he was carrying.

At the sight of Hen's face, Benjamin started to wail. He scooped up the child in spite of the heat burning his hands. Menachem tried to take her, but Benjamin hugged her to his chest, so Menachem dumped the remaining water on both of them.

"Why would anyone do this?" he whispered as he sank to the ground and Menachem knelt beside him. As he examined his daughter's body, he discovered a deep knife wound.

"Tova described the rites of Moloch to me one night when I woke her from a nightmare. She'd been screaming in her sleep. At least once a year Moloch's worshippers sacrifice a child, often the offspring of one of the temple prostitutes."

Benjamin regarded him in horror. "I've heard rumors of human sacrifice of course, but Judith and I never discussed it. I didn't think it was common."

"It is."

"But my Hen, she wasn't a prostitute's baby. She was beautiful, just like my Judith. Who would do such a thing?"

Menachem looked at him steadily. "Tova saw Judith racing down the other side of the hill."

Benjamin shuddered. "Why would Judith do such a thing?"

The Ammonite caravan appeared on the road to the east. Menachem watched it wend its way out of the village, "Because her heart has never belonged to Adonai."

Chapter 49

Oren looked up from his task of gathering dung for their cooking fires when he heard his name called. The voice sounded like his wife's, but the figure was approaching at a run, so it couldn't possibly be Jarah. She never ran. But he dropped his load and started back towards Gibeon and the runner.

Just as he recognized her tear-stained face and realized this *was* his wife, she stepped in a hole and fell to the rocky ground. Now *he* ran.

"Jarah, Jarah, are you hurt?" he cried, cradling her face between his dirty hands.

"Help me up, and I'll see." He pulled her up and supported her. "I'm all right, just winded. It's Naama. All the town has converged on the elders at the city gates, demanding she be stoned."

"Stoned! Why would they consider stoning anyone?"

"They say she stole Benjamin and Judith's baby and sacrificed her on that altar outside town."

"But it was pulled down!"

"Someone repaired it, but that's not important. An infant was burned there this morning."

"But why would they accuse Naama?"

"They're whispering about the loss of her baby, even questioning if Otanes was born alive and she killed him."

Oren stared in amazement.

"I know, I know. It's crazy, but they're whipping themselves into a frenzy. They may stone her before they figure out what happened. Can you get them to see reason? Hurry! Don't worry about me. I'll catch my breath and follow you."

Oren sprinted toward the city gates.

The gates were eerily empty. He continued through town. An infirm grandmother told him everyone had gone to Benjamin's vineyard. He sped up and shouldered his way through the shouting mob as he reached Ariel's. He feared they'd already killed her.

To his relief, he spied Naama huddled against the house, head down in her arms. Gili and Ariel stood in front of her brandishing swords. Although neither looked experienced with a sword, the crowd was unarmed and intimidated by the show of force.

"Stop, in the name of Ezra, who has appointed me a teacher in your village!" Oren shouted.

The mob quieted a bit and fell back a couple steps. The news of Oren's appointment had been announced as soon as the elders returned from their latest meeting with Ezra in Jerusalem. Oren strode into the area between the crowd and Ariel's beleaguered family. "What's all this about?"

"That woman," spat Carmela, "killed Benjamin's daughter on Moloch's altar."

"Did you see her do it?" Oren challenged.

Carmela shook her head.

"Did any of you see her kill a child?"

The crowd milled around and consulted each other, then pressed in closer to the house. "No, but that's two dead in a short time after being with *her*," an elder accused, pointing at Naama.

"For shame," Jarah yelled from the back of the crowd. "Naama's son was stillborn. I witnessed his birth with my own eyes. You would have too, if only you'd come to her aid," she added as she passed through the crowd to lay a hand on her friend's shoulder.

"Have any of you asked Naama where she was this morning?" Oren asked.

"She won't answer any of our questions," a middle-aged elder said. "Why won't she speak up if she's innocent?" A murmur of assent rippled through the villagers.

"She's barely eaten or spoken since our son died," Ariel said.

"And now you're cornering us and shouting at her."

"Naama, Naama, look at me," Jarah said soothingly. Slowly the young woman raised a grief-ravaged face toward her trusted friend. "Did you kill Hen, Benjamin and Judith's baby?"

"No, no! I was holding her yesterday while Judith prepared to leave. Such a beautiful baby! I could never do anything so wicked." She turned her eyes to the crowd, begging for their understanding.

Oren glared at the villagers. "As far as I can see, none of you has given Ariel's family a chance. They travelled all the way from Persia to come back to their ancestral land. The Persians treated them better than you, their own people have."

"If she didn't sacrifice Benjamin's baby, then who did?" yelled a man from the back of the crowd. The crowd began to murmur angrily.

"It's an abomination," another man shouted. "Whoever killed her should be stoned."

Oren signaled for quiet. "You know the law. There must be eyewitnesses."

"I saw Naama walking away from the spring toward the high place this morning," an unmarried girl said. "And she didn't carry a water pot."

Jarah looked into Naama's pain-filled eyes. "Why were you out that way so early?"

"I went to draw water. Ariel's been doing it, but I know I should be getting the water. I forgot my pot though." Naama's face burned with shame. "I wandered away, but I didn't go up the hill. Gili came and got the water."

Jarah ached for her friend and feared for her life, having known women who never recovered after losing babies. But Naama was young, and strong from the long trip earlier in the year. Surely, she could recover her health if these malicious villagers would cease their attack. "I believe you, Naama, and Adonai sees the truth. May He reveal it to your accusers."

"Di you see Naama at the high place or carrying Hen?" Oren sternly asked the teenager.

"No," she said sullenly.

"Anyone else have an accusation?" Oren demanded.

No one spoke, but the crowd inched forward with murderous intent.

Sweat broke out on Oren's brow as he tried unsuccessfully to make eye contact with one of the city elders. As the newest leader, his words did not carry enough weight to thwart the crowd's evil intent. He needed one of the elders to speak reason to these stubborn, backward people. *Please Adonai*, he begged as he took a step in front of Naama and his wife.

Another voice rang above the mob's buzz. "Judith sacrificed her own daughter."

Relief flooded Oren. "Let him through."

Menachem elbowed his way through the crowd. "Judith did this horrific thing. The elders knew she was a worshipper of Moloch. This is one more proof."

"How do you know? Did you see her do this horrible deed?" asked one of the elders skeptically.

"I did not see her, but I know."

"That still does not meet the requirements of an eyewitness," Oren said.

"I saw it," a soft voice said. Tova walked to the front of the throng, carrying Eliezer. "I saw Judith climbing the hill this morning. We've been friends since we were children, and I sensed trouble. I couldn't catch up to her because I carried Eliezer, but I got there in time to find Hen--" Tova gulped--"burning. She wasn't alive. She had a deep knife wound. Judith was disappearing down the other side of the hill. No one else was around."

The crowd fell back. "Wicked woman! Where is she?"

"Left with the caravan, no doubt."

"How do we know Tova is telling the truth? There is no other witness."

"Just Judith and she's gone."

"The caravan can't be far. Let's stop it and find out."

A score of young and middle-aged men peeled away from the

group, agreeing to meet to the east of town as soon as they could gather donkeys and fill water skins. One of the ancient elders said, "Where is the infant's body? We will examine it while you track down the mother."

Menachem took a wiggly Eliezer from his mother's arms. "Benjamin is mourning over his daughter. If you come with me, you'll see the evidence."

Oren joined the elder who had spoken. Menachem first stopped by his home, where he left his wife and son. Then he led them to the town's burial grounds, where they found Benjamin covered in ash, still clutching the disintegrating form of his baby girl. The smell made Oren want to retreat and retch, but he moved forward as the elder gently took the babe and examined the knife wound.

"This confirms part of Tova's story," he commented as he handed the baby back and rested his hands on Benjamin's shoulders. "You do not need to bury her alone, son. If you agree, I think tomorrow would be the best day to put her to rest. We all mourn with you."

Benjamin nodded briefly and turned away.

Chapter 50

Judith trailed behind the caravan. Her instincts screamed that the Jews would hunt her down. They abhorred human sacrifice and might try to punish her according to their law. She wanted to make it back to her family, but she would not return to be beaten.

She would offer herself to Adlai. *Please, Moloch, may he treat me well despite my desperate circumstances.* Since she possessed a few coins, she could buy food and make herself as attractive as possible before she faced him. If she could make him believe *she* had chosen *him,* it would go better for her. Hopefully he hadn't married since the beginning of the year. He wouldn't be inclined to take a second wife so quickly if he had.

Maybe another opportunity would present itself on the journey before she looked for Adlai. She must remain sharp, not dwell on Hen. Her gut twisted at the memory of her daughter, but she distracted herself with thoughts of Jericho—the excitement and bustle of a city on a major caravan route, the silk fabrics and brilliant jewels in the market.

Unable to recover the scout's body, the men insisted on lighting a fire and offering a sacrifice for their fallen comrade. Ctesias chafed at the delay, but he recognized stirrings of mutiny, so he joined the proceedings in a show of respect. *Ezra's daughter will recognize me if she sees me again. My men are good fighters, but the Jews outnumber us. If they position a few archers, they'll make retreat difficult and cause more casualties.*

The sun was high when their cavalcade set out. They rode hard and didn't encounter any problems. They were approaching Jericho and safety beyond the Jordan River when a scout called his attention to a lone woman trailing far behind a small caravan. He veered from the road to intercept her.

Judith was exhausted. Villagers from Gibeon had caught up with the caravan shortly after the morning respite. She suspected the spurned Ammonite women told them nothing, not even confirming whether Judith had started out with them in the morning. The merchants didn't know one woman from another and couldn't help the angry townspeople.

A few Gibeonites spread out to search the immediate terrain, but most headed straight back to Gibeon. *Fools.* The last Jew had turned back hours ago, but she was still skulking through the brush behind the caravan, just in case. She wasn't paying attention to the road to the south, just the one west toward Gibeon, so the mounted Persian drew close before she heard his steed. Knowing flight would be futile, she stopped and studied him.

"Going far?" he asked.

"No, not at all," Judith replied.

Ctesias detected only weariness, no fear in the woman's stance. "We're headed to Jericho," he offered, jerking his head toward a mounted band of Bactrians that followed him. "Could we escort you?"

Since the caravan was too far away to help, even if they chose, Judith knew he could do whatever he pleased with her. "That would be much appreciated," she said regally.

"Is your family with the caravan?" the Persian asked, Judith walking as he rode beside her.

"No."

"You might as well ride, if you've a mind to."

Judith considered the impropriety of riding with a man unrelated to her, but his offer was tempting. She *was* tired since she had been awake most of last night. This could be the opportunity she had wanted. "I've been walking all day. I'd like to ride."

When the Persian swung her up behind him, she scooted close to his muscled back. *This man might be the answer to my predicament.*

"Hold on," he invited, "Jaspar spooks occasionally."

Judith immediately snaked an arm around the man's belly. Fire coursed through her body at the man's scent and sinew. He reached back and positioned her other arm securely around his midsection.

She would spend the night with this man. Maybe she'd spend the rest of her nights with him. He looked wealthy, good cloth for robe and tunic. He was the leader of this entourage, and his stallion was obviously expensive. Sleepily she wondered what these horsemen were doing in Yehud. Perhaps they had sold some animals and were headed home. Or he could be a merchant, though she didn't see any pack animals.

Where is home for him? Home... I have no home, no protection, nothing but my small bundle, which my "rescuer" tossed to an underling. I need to make the best of this night.

∞∞∞

The villagers of Gibeon returned from hunting Judith tired and dusty, but still bloodthirsty and angry. Before dinnertime, new gossip spread like a plague of locusts. Why was Tova going up to the high place this morning? Was she really following Judith? Or was she already on her way to worship when she realized someone was in front of her? After all, she was an Ammonite just like Judith.

Jarah overheard the alarming talk among children playing on the street. They were playing hide-and-seek, but only one child hid while the others searched for the "Ammonite." They carried sticks and stones to beat her when they found her. Fearing the children would hurt each other, Jarah broke up their game and sent them home. Then she hurried to Menachem and Tova's house.

"Shalom," Tova greeted her.

"Not today," Jarah answered. "Gather what you need. I think you should stay elsewhere tonight. Let's be ready to go when Menachem returns."

"Why?"

"These people are suspicious of you now."

"That's been going on for a while."

"They're asking if you were going to worship at the high place this morning when you saw Judith."

"But I explained..."

"I know, I know, but the hotheads didn't find Judith, and they want to punish someone. Let's make sure it's not you."

When Menachem returned, Oren accompanied him. "You've already heard the rumors?" Menachem asked grimly. The women nodded. "We think the best place to go is Naama's, so there will be three men. We'll be out of town so not as accessible, and we can post a lookout. Oren and Jarah will stay in town and listen for trouble."

As soon as it was dark, Menachem's family slipped out of the house and made their way to Ariel's small abode.

Ctesias liked this woman. She was lovely and had great presence of mind. Although she lay in his power like a deer before a lion, she behaved like a queen. It had been so long since he'd taken a woman. Tonight would be full of pleasure. He was pleased when he felt her rest against his back, her breathing slow and regular. *Sleep now, my beauty. Tonight we have other business.*

He motioned four of the men to enter Jericho and buy food while the rest set up camp to the east of the city along the Jordan River. The small caravan had already disappeared into the bustling city. He called a man to lift the girl down and then dismounted. She looked younger than he had first thought. When she stirred, he said gently, "Rest for now. I'll bring you food soon."

She was alert and had washed off the day's dust in the river when he returned with bread and dried meat.

"Could I have my bundle? There's a skin of water in it."

Ctesias sent one of the younger men to fetch it. "Here have some of mine while you wait." Ctesias held it to her lips and let his eyes linger on her face. "What's your name?"

"Judith."

"And how did you come to be trailing a caravan across Judea?"

Judith stopped eating and looked down.

He gently lifted her chin. Her eyes and perfect face appealed to him far more than his wife's. It was time for a second wife. "You can trust me."

"What's your name?"

"Ctesias."

"You're Persian?"

"Yes."

"Do you live in Persia?"

"Yes."

The young woman seemed to relax. "I don't like Jews," she said with vehemence.

"You aren't a Jew?" he asked.

"No, are you disappointed?" she asked coyly.

Ctesias rolled onto his back and looked at the stars. "Not at all, not at all. Actually I hate Jews, but having found you walking across Israel's plains, I assumed…"

"I'm Ammonite."

"I like you better already."

Judith's silvery laugh caused the men pitching a tent nearby to turn and stare.

"Back to work," Ctesias commanded.

Judith dropped her eyes and attention back to her food. When he rolled over to study her in the fire's light, he sucked in his breath. She'd removed her veil and was daintily licking her fingers. Thick hair framed her face. His gaze dropped lower. The front of her dress had two dark spots forming where the curves of her breasts met the fabric. She stirred uncomfortably under his scrutiny.

As Judith had rested and eaten, her milk started flowing. *Not the picture I'm trying to present.* She blushed and tried to turn her body from him. He reached out to prevent her. "You have a babe?"

Pain seared Judith. She pushed it away, "Not anymore."

Ctesias didn't press for details. After a moment, he grinned. "I could help you."

Judith ducked her head and said alluringly, "I bet you could."

Ctesias rose and guided her toward his tent.

Chapter 51

Later that night, Ctesias examined his prize more carefully as she slept. Her body had taken him places he didn't know existed, to Paradise and back. She still had a rounded belly from having a child recently, but he was sure it would tighten. She would be perfect. He would plant his seed in her, and she would bear him many strong sons. He would not return to Susa empty-handed after all.

With Judith, he could found a dynasty. She hated the Jews because one had divorced her for worshipping Moloch. She had explained with a defiance that thrilled him. The Jews had kept her dowry too. It was perfect, absolutely perfect.

He lay back down and nuzzled her neck. Stirring, she arched and murmured, "More?"

He sensed the smile in her voice.

"You were married to a Jew, weren't you? How did you learn..." he began when he could catch his breath.

"At the festivals to Moloch I became skilled in the ways of pleasing a man."

"Skilled? You're a goddess. I'm never letting you go. What were you going to do once you returned home?"

"I had a few plans, but...I'd like to hear yours."

"I plan to make you the head wife of my house."

"So I'm not the only one?"

Ctesias heard the pout in Judith's voice. "My other wife is old. Of course, I had never seriously considered taking another wife until I met you. But she's quite old and often unhealthy. You would rule my household. I have a comfortable estate in Susa and a flourishing import business."

"Are you here in Judah to trade?"

"No, other business."

Judith traced her fingers along his chest and shoulders. "So I wouldn't have to work in a vineyard?"

"Absolutely not. I own a cadre of servants too, Greeks, Parthians." He caught her delicate yet roughened hand. "Your hands will be the soft hands of a rich woman, decked with jewels."

"And what will I do for you?" Judith asked playfully.

"Nothing but this. And of course bear our children as the gods bless us."

"Bearing children is risky work, my lord."

What had happened to her child? Had it sickened and died? "You shall have your heart's desire after each delivery," he promised with a kiss.

"What if I lust for something other than cloth and jewels?"

"Then you're a rare woman indeed. What would you desire?"

"Besides your strength and closeness?"

"Ah, flattery. But yes, what else?"

"The head of the Jew Benjamin son of Isaak, villager of Gibeon."

Ctesias blinked. "And what did this man do to incur the wrath of my goddess?"

"He let them send me away." Judith's voice caught, and Ctesias detected her anguish.

"So this man is responsible for my finding you today?"

"Yes."

Ctesias enfolded her in his arms. "I feel I owe him a great debt."

"He hurt me."

Ctesias made a great show of examining her. "You're perfection itself. I can't see that he's laid a hand on you."

"There are hurts that go more than skin deep, my lord."

"Yes," Ctesias agreed thoughtfully. "I have no issue killing a Jew. I'll do it with pleasure for you." Ctesias held her closely. "As a matter of fact, since we're here and I already have the assassins, would you like his head now, to seal the pledge I make to you?"

Judith turned in his arms, dark eyes glowing. "I'll be yours forever," she whispered.

The moon was setting an hour later when Ctesias said, "Sleep now while I send my men to fulfill your request. You'll be tired on our journey tomorrow."

"Can't I sleep while we ride your stallion?"

"Always, but I need a few hours rest."

"As you wish." Judith rolled over and nestled into the rough blankets as though they were silk.

Ctesias admired her as he pulled on a tunic and sheathed his knife. He woke three men and sent them to find Benjamin. "If possible, bring him to me alive."

Hadassah was being chased by a menacing Persian and his army. She had outrun them all the way to the Jordan River, but was trapped like a sheep hunted by lions. She jerked awake from her dream as the men reached her.

Glad she had lit an oil lamp before she and Adin lay down to sleep, Hadassah shivered in fear. Her father said a group camped outside Jerusalem had left. They were probably the riffraff who threatened her and wouldn't be seen again, but she was to stay in the temple compound.

Hadassah sighed. She was thankful for her sister's presence but wished for Jarah's company. *I was happy again before I was attacked. Now I'm afraid to leave my room.*

But Jarah would say Adonai had protected her. She was written on the palm of His hand, and He hadn't forgotten her. He had been there when she needed Him the most. Hadassah relaxed. It was true. Adonai had been there in her hour of need. Those evil foreigners hadn't caught her. Adonai had also been there when Jedidiah died. It was she who had not reached out for His comfort.

Ezra fasted and prayed in the next room. *God of Abraham, Isaac, and Jacob, I praise You for Your protection on our long journey here from the land of our captivity. Yet even here our enemies harass us and plot against us and our children.* Ezra swallowed a lump in his throat as he pictured Hadassah. *Thank You for delivering my daughter, my firstborn, from the wicked men who pursued her. Although her body bears no injury, her spirit suffers many wounds. Please give my girl peace and a sense of safety and security. I thank You again for protecting her.*

And please, Adonai, protect the Jews scattered throughout this land and the empire. May we bring glory to Your great name. We have put away our foreign wives. Bless those men who have chosen to follow You by giving them new families. I think especially of the young man from Gibeon who believed his wife followed You. The elders did not agree, and I sanctioned their divorce. My heart is heavy for him tonight, and I fear for him. Watch over him, Adonai.

Chapter 52

Silent shadows, three Bactrian assassins crept into Gibeon over the town's walls. Two located a sentry and forced him to divulge the location of Benjamin's home before knocking him unconscious with a stout shepherd's rod.

The boy huddled in the shadows while men clubbed his father. He had fallen asleep in the third watch. His father's cry had roused him, but he remained still until the attackers set off for Benjamin's. Had they killed his father? He inched over to the body and brought his face close. No, he could feel his father's breath on his cheek, but his head was sticky with blood. David ran to find his Uncle Enoch, husband of Benjamin's youngest sister Mary. He would know what to do for David's father and Benjamin.

Breathless, he pounded on his uncle's door, glad the vineyard was the other way. "Quickly, uncle. Men came and clubbed father. They're on their way to Benjamin's." As his sleepy aunt drew David into the house, his wiry uncle grabbed a staff and sheathed a knife. David eyed him dubiously. "They were big and fierce. You'll need more men."

Another knock sounded at the door. Enoch opened it to Oren, his neighbor. "Is there trouble, Enoch? We heard a ruckus."

"Some men attacked the sentry and are going to Benjamin's."

"Mary, take my wife to tend the sentry. Boy, rouse more men and send them armed to Benjamin's," Oren said. "Let's get to the vineyard. What's the fastest way?"

"It'll be rough going in the dark. Take a torch," Enoch said, thrusting one into the fire. Grabbing the oil lamp from the table, he set off behind the house toward a small gate in the thick city walls. Oren grabbed the torch and followed.

As they reached the path approaching the vineyard, they heard shouts and the clang of swords. Breaking into a run and lifting their lights high, they dashed into the clearing around Benjamin's stone cottage. Three Bactrians had backed a man with a sword against the house.

Two men in loincloths ran into the circle of light from the opposite direction. A knife glinted in Menachem's hand as he thrust it into the nearest assassin's back.

Joining the melee, Enoch raised his staff and brought it down over the head of another.

Ariel closed in on the remaining fighter. "Leave us alone," he cried as he plunged it into his neck.

Oren, who had avoided the fight since he was unarmed, opened Benjamin's door with a feeling of dread. Broken bits of pottery crunched under his sandals. What had these murderers done to the grieving man? After perusing the room for a body, he righted a stool and exited.

"Where's Benjamin?"

"I don't know," Gili said, chest heaving from the fight. "I called for his help, but when he didn't answer, I yelled for Ariel. Good thing you all came when you did." He fingered a bleeding bicep.

Naama and Tova entered the circle of torchlight, carrying Eliezer, rags and a pitcher of water. Naama gently began cleaning the wound.

"Why did we come here?" Ariel asked, surveying the body at his feet. "Nothing but trouble. We're not safe. Naama's not safe."

"Naama?" Enoch asked.

"Yes. We figured someone might come back to exact 'justice' for the death of the babies. We've been taking turns keeping watch," Gili explained.

"Praise Adonai!" Enoch thundered. "But look at these men. They're not Jews who wished to harm your wife."

"I'd say from their dress they're Bactrians. At any rate, they sneaked into the city and assaulted the sentry, extracting information about Benjamin's whereabouts," Oren added.

"But why?" Ariel asked shakily.

"We don't know."

"Doesn't look like we'll find out from them." Gili nudged the nearest body with his foot.

"We need to find Benjamin," Enoch said. "There may be more assassins."

"Let's try the gravesites. Maybe he never left," Oren offered. "Will you be all right?" he asked the wounded man.

Gili looked to Ariel, who crouched on the ground with a dazed look on his face. "We're safer out here than we'd be in town," Gili finally said.

Enoch squatted down to look into Ariel's face. "You are one of us now. No one will harm your wife. I swear it. Thank you for protecting my brother."

Ariel nodded numbly.

Naama tried to help her husband rise after the men left.

"I'm unclean. I've never killed a man," Ariel lamented, motioning her away.

Naama put her arms around him. "You had no choice. They were here on a mission to kill. You saved Gili. And you thought... you both thought they were here to hurt me. You were fighting for me." There was awe in her voice. She kissed his forehead. "We will build a life here. Someday we'll have many sons, and we will find Gili a wife so he can enjoy the same. All will be well, husband. Come back to our home."

Naama led her husband and his wounded cousin back across the vineyard. Menachem and Tova followed with Eliezer.

Chapter 53

I'm sorry, precious. My men couldn't bring back Benjamin's head." Ctesias avoided telling her all three men were dead. "They killed him," he fibbed, "but other Jews showed up and drove them off before they could separate his body from his head."

Ctesias had sent more men at the break of day to discover what happened to the first three. Gibeon was crawling with armed men, but they crept around to the west of the city where carrion birds circled a quiet vineyard. They discovered their cousins' bodies, but several people were moving around among the vines, so they quickly returned to camp. Ctesias tried to gauge Judith's reaction to the news.

"As long as he's dead," she said with a toss of her thick hair, but Ctesias didn't detect any satisfaction or joy.

"How fast can you be ready to leave? As you can imagine, we need to disappear."

Judith belted her robe. "Just let me go down to the river."

Her thoughts spun as she washed her hands and face in the Jordan. She would never see her family again. She shuddered as she pictured Benjamin cradling Hen, a look of pure joy on his face. *How could he send us away? He never loved us. Now I have a much stronger man, a leader, someone who will never leave me.*

She rubbed the idol around her neck and hurried back to the camp, which had been completely dismantled. The men mounted when they saw her, except for one youngster leading a chestnut filly.

Ctesias rode up to her on his magnificent black stallion. "You'll be more comfortable on your own mount than riding behind me all day. We need to cover as many parasangs as possible. If you tire later, you can ride with me."

Judith stepped into the young man's cupped hands and swung onto her mount. She tried to adjust her dress to cover her legs, but it only reached to the knee. She thanked the gods Adlai had taught her to ride.

As the band set out, she fell into line near the rear. She remembered her first ride on a horse. She had often ridden her family's donkey as she took bread and figs to her brothers while they tended the goats. One sultry day she found her favorite brother Tobiah enjoying a visit with one of his friends.

Adlai came from a wealthy family and had ridden a bay filly to the countryside west of Rabbah to see Tobiah. In spite of his wealth, Adlai didn't have many friends. Most of the Ammonite youth worked hard on farms or herding animals. They enjoyed contests of strength and endurance at the festivals throughout the year. Adlai was pudgy and couldn't win at any of the young men's games. Besides his chubbiness, Adlai's arm and leg had been scarred in a fire, so physically there was little to recommend him. But Adlai treated Judith with kindness. Tobiah said he was sweet on Judith, but Judith didn't care the reason. She made it clear she wasn't interested in a husband yet while lapping up the attention Adlai offered.

On that particular day she jumped off the donkey, scolding him for his stubbornness, and handed Tobiah his lunch. "I brought you extra so there should be plenty for Adlai too." As the teens wolfed down the meal, she rubbed Adlai's mount between the eyes.

Adlai finished and strode over to her. "She likes you. Do you want to ride her?"

Judith was thrilled. Usually only the men rode horses. "Yes," she cried in delight.

"Put your foot in my hands, and I'll boost you up." Without hesitation, Judith did as he said and found herself perched on a blanket on the horse's sleek back.

"She's much more responsive than a mule, so guide her gently with the reins," Adlai instructed.

Judith walked the horse to the edge of the rocky field where the goats grazed and back until the sun's shadows warned her she'd soon be late. She had to whip the cantankerous donkey to hurry back to their tents, but she didn't regret the time she'd spent on the filly.

Judith often found Adlai with her brother after her first ride. She brought extra food for him, and he let her walk and trot his horse. A couple times he galloped as Judith clung to his waist.

Those days ended abruptly when her father announced her marriage to Benjamin. The family had experienced difficulties finding a reliable vinedresser in Gibeon, so her father saw the arrangement as the perfect solution. Benjamin would care for the troublesome vineyard. It would be Judith's dowry, so her marriage would cost the family very little beyond the marriage feast. Benjamin's family had lived in Gibeon for generations and was pleased for their third son to marry into property since they didn't have enough land for all four sons.

This solution pleased everyone, except Judith, who didn't know what to think. She had pictured herself as the wife of a well-to-do merchant in a city. Now she would end up working in a vineyard, but her concerns were settled when she met Benjamin.

He had journeyed to Rabbah and was introduced by his older brother, who had settled there with an Ammonite wife. Benjamin was one of the most handsome men Judith had ever laid eyes on. His gentle manner completely won her over. In all the years of their marriage, he had never raised his voice or his hand to her.

Judith shook herself. How did thinking about horses and Adlai lead to Benjamin? He was her past. Her eyes sought her future, settling on Ctesias' powerful back. He wasn't as handsome as Benjamin had been, but he was strong, not weak. He would never let anyone come between them, not even his wife. Judith smiled in triumph. She hoped his wife would adjust with a minimum of fuss. It would help for her to present Ctesias with a son, but it wouldn't do to become pregnant before the journey's end.

Chapter 54

J oiada examined the ornate box. He had come to the chamber of wood in the temple to make sure it was stocked and had discovered three boxes half his height, carved with pomegranates. They were probably for the new bet 'ammas, but why? Two doors opened at the front to reveal a storage space. He noted that the chamber was half full and turned to leave and ask his father about the boxes.

David was standing behind him, grinning. "Aren't they beautiful? The artisans who learned their craft in Susa and Babylon do fine work, don't they?"

"What are they?"

"Arks."

"Arks!! Now he's putting an *ark* in each bet 'amma? There's only one ark, and it was lost in the Babylonians' pillaging. I need to go tell father what he's doing."

"Wait," David said, laying a hand on his arm. "Of course there's only one ark of the covenant. These arks are to protect the scrolls the scribes are copying for each village."

"What?"

"They're to protect the scrolls, not house God's presence."

"Why not use an earthen pot or put them on a shelf?"

"This is the way it's done in Persia." David considered the beautifully carved furniture. "I think it's to convey how important God's words are, to bring a feeling of worship." He gestured around the clean, gilt temple, ending at Joiada's brilliant new robe. "Our God loves beauty."

Joiada sank onto a nearby bench and hung his head. "I misunderstood."

"There's a lot of that going on here lately." David sat beside his brother. "I overheard something interesting the other day."

Joiada remained slumped, staring at the ground.

"You will be our next leader, brother. What you're becoming today is what you'll be tomorrow."

"God help us all, eh?" Joiada muttered.

"You're the one who said it, not me."

Joiada sighed and propped himself up on his elbows. "What did you hear?"

"I overheard one of Ezra's daughters talking to him. She was expressing her opinion of you," David paused, considering his brother. "What did you do to the youngest girl?"

"We had a misunderstanding."

"Whatever the *misunderstanding* was, her sister compared you to a rat."

Joiada groaned. "Why are you telling me this?"

"Because of her father's response. He said, 'Joiada will be our next high priest. He made a mistake with Adin, but he deserves our respect.'"

Joiada looked at his brother in amazement.

"There's more. The woman started saying he should be the next high priest, but her father said he's there to teach the people God's law, not take on the high priest's duties. He said he needed to focus on the one thing Adonai gave him to do.

"She asked if one of their husbands could take on those responsibilities. His status as the high priest's father would give greater weight to his words."

"What'd Ezra say?" Joiada demanded sourly.

"He said, 'Joiada will be the next high priest. He's been training for the position his whole life. We have lived our lives in exile and don't know the temple procedures.' She said at least they have good hearts. Ezra answered that only God knows the heart. She also said you'd forfeited high position because of your wife's family. He said that made no difference."

"He did? I've wondered how others would view my wife's relatives. Are you sure they didn't know you were listening?"

"They couldn't see me on the other side of the fence. They were talking on the stone steps in front of the main temple gates."

"Not a good place for a private chat since the sound carries. Remember how much fun our sons had yelling while they played on the steps right after they were finished?"

"Until abba set them straight about their behavior."

"They thought since they were *outside* the gates, they could do as they pleased."

"Abba told them to stop behaving like heathen. The steps were just as sacred as the rest of the temple."

"They were little boys. They just didn't understand...maybe I just didn't understand."

"God gives wisdom to those who ask," David reminded, clapping him on the back.

"I'd better start asking."

Chapter 55

Oren pried the charred baby from Benjamin's grip while two of Ben's brothers restrained him. Benjamin's mother gently took the tiny bundle and wrapped her in burial cloths. At least she would look like any other babe who died in infancy.

Oren feared for Benjamin's sanity. He had fought his family yesterday when they arrived at his house and tried to prepare Hen for burial. The women retreated, agreeing to give him another day to hold the remains of his daughter. But today the decaying body must be interred in the family tomb.

Now Benjamin collapsed on the rocky turf in front of his home, muttering incoherently and shaking off his brothers' hands. Silently, they crouched an arm's length away.

Oren returned to Gibeon to announce the imminence of the funeral and fetch an elder to speak over the child's grave. Jarah would meet him at the tombs when she left Naama's home. Oren's heart ached for Benjamin. To father a child, and then have the child's mother take her life was unthinkable! He hoped the elder's words of comfort would soothe Benjamin's soul.

When he told the elders at the city gate that the mourners would meet at the tombs shortly, most mumbled excuses about taking care of pressing business. A few broke away from the group. The elder who examined the babe two days previously rose on arthritic legs and surveyed the others sadly. Oren offered him a supporting arm, and they picked their way carefully to the bleak valley where shallow tombs were cut into vine-covered hillsides.

Benjamin was quiet, shoulders slumped, head hanging. His eldest brother emerged from the cave. He had placed the child's body inside, afraid to return the bundle to her father. His large family clustered around him. Another brother stood with his hands on the shoulders of his two children. Mary and Enoch stood close to her mother, who held Benjamin's arm.

A group of women cried across from the family. At the front of the group, Jarah, Naama, and Tova leaned on each other for support. When Tova swayed, Jarah took Eliezer, and Naama slipped an arm around her waist.

Menachem stood with Ariel and Gili and two elders who had managed to come.

Where is this town's compassion? And to think I'm now their teacher! Oren led the elder to the open tomb. The man sighed and turned to face the mourners.

"Life is short, my friends." He paused. "Especially for this little one." He wiped a tear from his cheek. "I think of another innocent child. Our father David said this upon his death, 'I will go to him, but he will not return to me.' You will see your daughter again, Benjamin. There is life beyond what we can see with our eyes. As I grow old, I sense it more and more with my spirit. Now we commit this child to Adonai, who formed her."

"Amen," said those assembled.

"Amen."

Another elder moved forward to aid the ancient, who shuffled to Benjamin and put his hands on his shoulders, "I pray every day for you, my son. Come see me if there's anything I can do for you."

Benjamin nodded, and the elders went back to Gibeon.

Oren joined Jarah and reached for Eliezer. It looked like Menachem might have to carry Tova home. She was distraught, kneeling by Benjamin and his mother while his brothers and their sons covered the tomb with two large rocks.

Ariel and Gili flanked Naama and quietly turned towards home. As contenders for Benjamin's vineyard, they had shown respect for their neighbor but would not become an unwelcome presence when the mourners went back to the house and villagers brought food.

Oren hoped the Gibeonites would extend that courtesy to their suffering countryman. *Regardless of their feelings for Judith, surely they'll embrace this young man who grew up here, won't they? Or will they ignore him as the women ignored Naama in her hour of need?*

He carried Eliezer to their home so Jarah could collect bread and a pot of stew she had left simmering. They would return the boy to his parents on their way to Benjamin's. Tova had walked to the city gates before collapsing. Her husband tenderly gathered her in his arms and carried her home.

∞∞∞

The horses forded the high water of the Jordan without incident. Judith changed her mind about the length of her robes being too short and pulled them higher to keep them from being muddied. It would be a long day of riding, with many days or weeks of travel to reach Ctesias' home. *Did he tell me where he lived? Never mind. It's far away from the Jews, which is all that matters.*

Drawing on Judith's knowledge of the area, Ctesias had headed along the road to Rabbah. Trade routes wound through the Ammonite's former capital to the north, south, east, and northeast. He consulted with his men and chose the northerly route through Damascus. The group would then head to Tadmor.

Although sore the first few days, Judith adjusted to the horse's gait. Her milk dried up quickly, and she forced memories of Hen away. She focused on the future, teasing Ctesias at night for descriptions of his fine house and courtyard, which were in Susa. It sounded larger than the best merchant homes in Rabbah. The king and queen resided in Susa during the winter, and Ctesias occasionally went to the palace on business or for a banquet.

I hope I can visit the palace and admire its luxuries. It will be amazing to manage a household with servants and be able to enjoy society rather than grub in a vineyard.

Every night she implored Moloch for a good start for her new life. She regretted being unable to send word to her family about her relocation, but it couldn't be helped. She would try to remedy the situation after she was installed in her new home.

After the Bactrians settled at an inn near the souk at Damascus' main gate, Ctesias told Judith they had better accommodations. She mounted her filly, and two guards accompanied them along the city's streets to a wealthy part of the town. Towering palms topped stone walls with protected courtyards.

When they stopped at an intricately carved wooden gate, the gatekeeper immediately swung it open and greeted Ctesias with a low bow. Another servant hurried to alert his master of "the noble Ctesias' arrival" while young girls washed Judith and Ctesias' feet. A portly merchant bustled into the courtyard, followed by a significantly younger and more attractive wife and a teenaged son.

Judith and Ctesias were soon ensconced in a large bedchamber complete with bed and two couches and a view of the inner courtyard's fountain and flowers. As soon as the two had washed away the travel grime and dined on pork and pomegranates with their host, Ctesias closed the door, shutting out the view, and took Judith directly to bed.

∞∞∞∞

Judith was sorry to leave Damascus after only two nights of rest at the merchant's home. Ctesias assured her that once they reached Mari, they would be halfway home, and Tadmor would be another pleasant city en route to Mari.

Tired of the dry mountainous region, Judith became excited

two days before their intended arrival at the city of trade, but she was surprised the Bactrians seemed to share her enthusiasm. They had seemed unimpressed by Damascus, which was larger than Tadmor.

Late in the afternoon Ctesias left his position at the head of the cavalcade and moved her to the rear, which displeased her due to the increased dust. "It's safer here. Our scouts have located a small merchant caravan. The caravan's not going to reach the caravansary before dark, so my men are going to surprise them after dusk and loot them. If the merchants and their guards resist, there may be bloodshed. No matter what happens, stay back so a stray arrow or runaway guard won't harm you."

Noting her expression, Ctesias continued, "It wasn't my plan to attack caravans, but the men are disappointed we couldn't steal the temple treasures in Jerusalem. I can't have them turning on us or deserting us. There's strength in numbers in the desert. Too many marauders, both animal and human."

Judith wanted to grab his arm and hear assurances that all would be well, but Ctesias had galloped back to the front. The Bactrians became silent, intent on surprising their prey, and she rode in their wake, hating the dust blowing in her eyes. Thankfully, her veil protected her nose and mouth. They rode longer than any other day, and she was ready to fall from the saddle as darkness fell.

She couldn't see anything but heard shouts and cursing. *It's begun.* She reined up her mount and waited, hidden in the darkness. A few stars winked in the sky before she saw men or horses advancing toward her. They rushed past. Puzzled, she turned. Realization that Ctesias' men were running away hit her with a sickening force. She turned the filly and let her run with the mob.

Judith saw one man fall after an arrow pierced his neck. She bent low over the filly's neck and urged her to more speed with her knees. Prickles of terror raised the hairs on her neck as she heard their pursuers shouting in Aramaic. Perhaps if she split off from the main group and hid in an arroyo, she could escape, but she couldn't see to guide her mount in the dark. The filly might turn her leg in a crevice.

Judith rubbed the idol at her breast and breathed prayers to Moloch for safety. With relief, she heard the familiar scream of Ctesias' battle stallion. *Ctesias will rescue me.* But he galloped past, bareheaded. He would undoubtedly escape since his stallion could outrun them all.

A parasang later, her horse slowed, and a rider vaulted off his camel and knocked her to the ground. The weight on her back reminded Judith of the lion that had attacked her in the vineyard. Benjamin had rescued her that time, but no one would save her now. She waited for the sharp blade of a knife in her back or at her neck, but her assailant paused and pulled off her head covering. "This one's a woman," he shouted, beginning to push up her robe over her hips. With his other hand he flipped her onto her back.

"Hold," a strong voice called from the darkness.

Stunned and winded by the fall and rough treatment, Judith caught a glimpse of the speaker and screamed. The face illumined by a torch was her dead husband.

Chapter 56

Judith regained consciousness slowly. She felt a silky covering over her. Her head felt like a smith was pounding it on his anvil. Her back and shoulders ached. It hurt to take a deep breath. She tried moving her right foot. It responded. She wiggled her left foot. Pain shot up her leg. What had happened?

She relaxed in the soft cushions, trying to remember. The face! It had been Benjamin's face, but aged, with streaks of gray in his curly, dark hair. She must have been hallucinating, because of her panic and the memory of her earlier rescue from the lion. After all, he was dead. Her heart filled with remorse. He would never grow old because she had asked Ctesias to kill him.

Ctesias, bah! What a coward! She wanted to spit on him. *Is Moloch punishing me?* Her head spun, and she closed her eyes. A slave girl slipped into the dark tent and dribbled water into her mouth. Judith swallowed greedily. The girl spoke to her in words she didn't understand. *Is my brain addled?*

The girl left and returned shortly with a man. It was the man who had carried the light. Although his hair was covered with the traditional head covering, Judith panicked. *Am I dead? That was the only way this older version of Benjamin and I could exist in the same sphere. But if I'm dead, why does my head throb?*

"Don't be frightened," the man said calmly, in a voice like Benjamin's. "I'm not going to hurt you. I had the man who was… uh…*handling* you flogged. I'm a God-fearer. I don't allow women to be dishonored on the caravans I lead." He settled himself cross-legged a respectful distance from Judith's pallet.

"It seems you are part of my caravan now. The men you were with are dead or scattered. My name is Dael, son of Isaak. I'm a merchant travelling from Tadmor to Rabbah, where I live with my wife and five children."

The throbbing in Judith's head abated. *Dael! Benjamin's older brother who arranged their marriage. This explained his resemblance to Benjamin.* She had never met him. He had spoken with her father and brother Tobiah to arrange the bride price, but his wife had been ill when the marriage was celebrated, so they had not attended. But what could she tell him? Her marriage was over. Benjamin was dead.

"Brother," she rasped. Pausing, she signaled the slave for more water. After taking several swallows, she tried again. "I thought I was seeing a ghost. Your deceased brother Benjamin resembled you. I am his widow Judith. I believe you spoke to my family to arrange our marriage. He was a good man..." her voice broke. She had betrayed him and taken up with a coward instead.

Dael bowed his head sadly and grasped his tunic, ripping it with strong hands. "Did the rabble who attacked my caravan kill him and carry you off?"

Close enough to the truth. Judith nodded.

"I grieve with you, my sister. Do you think you could travel today if I arrange a litter for you? It will be safer if we can reach the caravansary before dark. It isn't far. We can resume our trip to Damascus when you've recovered."

"Yes. I ache all over. I'd appreciate a litter."

"It will be done. Rest now."

∞∞∞

The trip to the caravansary only covered a parasang of distance but hurt more than anything Judith had experienced. Her hands and face were scraped and sensitive, so Dael ordered servants to carry an awning over her while strong guards took turns bearing the litter. She was vaguely aware of being carried through the huge gate and into a cool, dim room before darkness claimed her.

Dael's caravan stayed for two nights before pushing on towards Damascus. Judith managed to ride her filly, which Dael's men had caught after the failed raid. Just before dusk the caravan took shelter in a caravansary along the Barada River. Judith settled into the well-protected corner of a large room housing Dael's group and one other merchant train.

Two nights later she rose and limped toward the women's facilities, leaving the girl who served as her maid sleeping soundly. When she emerged from the small room, a figure materialized from the shadows surrounding the building. "Are you all right?"

Judith recognized the voice she had heard in the darkness during many nights of pleasure. "Battered and bruised but all right, no thanks to you and those hare-brained Bactrians."

"I couldn't help you at the time, but I've come back for you. My men wanted to hightail it for home."

I can scream and be done with Ctesias, or I can rejoin him and hope we reach Susa and his home safely. If I continue to travel with Dael, I'll end up in Rabbah, with Adlai or at my family's mercy. I know now the kind of man Ctesias is... but he did backtrack to find me.

She didn't relish the idea of rejoining the Bactrians. She prized her life, and they had seriously miscalculated before their last escapade. "What about your men?"

Ctesias cursed. "There are only two left. The rest scattered or were killed. If we wait here in Damascus with my friend Aram, we can join a caravan to Susa. One of my own caravans should pass through sometime in the next moon, which would give you ample time to recover. Staying with Aram will be pleasant. You could have your own room if you wish," Ctesias persisted.

Judith hesitated, trying to make him think she had options, though he was the best choice by far. "My brother's been good to me," she began.

"Brother?"

"Dael, the master of the caravan you attacked, was Benjamin's older brother. He arranged our marriage."

Ctesias' gut clenched. *Would Judith return with Dael and discover Benjamin still lived?* He relaxed. *If she does, it won't make a difference. I'll be on the other side of the empire. Though I'd hate to lose her.*

"How would I leave Dael's care? He wants to return me to my family near Rabbah."

"Can't you simply leave while your brother and his men are about their business tomorrow?"

"He's given me a maid who follows me everywhere. If I want to go to the market or somewhere else in the city at least one guard will accompany us. He's pledged to keep me safe until he returns me to my family." Judith sighed. *So much like Benjamin in his desire to protect me, at least until recently.* She waited while Ctesias formulated a plan.

"How about if I had several large grain jars delivered here tomorrow afternoon? Could you crawl into one? I'd come with a drover to collect them right before the gates are closed for the night. No one will notice us with all the activity at that time of night."

"I'd be missed right away as everyone settled down for the night."

"You're right," Ctesias admitted, admiration in his voice. "How about if I have them delivered tomorrow and you crawl into one of them early the next morning? I'll pick them up as soon as the caravans leave in the morning."

"Your plan could work. How will I recognize the jars?"

"I'll tie a black cord around the lip of one. I don't know what pattern they'll be decorated with, but I'll find three that are the same. You can crawl into the one marked with the rope." Ctesias hesitated. "You move like you're sore. Is anything broken?"

"Maybe a rib," Judith admitted.

"Traveling in a pithos won't be comfortable."

"Dael's talking of leaving soon. This whole affair has already held up his caravan. We'd better leave the day after tomorrow. I feel a little better every day."

"Good. I'll put a couple small pillows and a rug in the jar. If you crawl in at dawn, I'll come into the compound when the gates are opened. As soon as we clear the caravansary, we'll hide in a deserted alley and get you out of the jug." Ctesias clasped her hand and moved away.

"Thank you. For coming back."

Ctesias paused. "You're a treasure. It would be hard to leave you."

Judith smiled into the darkness.

The next day Judith rested on her pallet as much as possible, gathering strength for her flight. She regretted leaving a man as kind as Dael, but it couldn't be helped. *He'll hate me soon enough when he discovers the divorce and Benjamin's murder. Surely the villagers link me with Benjamin's demise, especially after the baby's.* Judith pushed the thoughts away and focused on her future.

When the first faint light streaked the horizon, Judith visited the facilities. Yesterday afternoon she had noted three clay pots positioned nearby. Black stallions galloped in a band around the center of each. One was tipped on its side and marked with black hemp.

After removing a soft sheepskin and two pillows, she shimmied in feet first and arranged the padding for more comfort. It wasn't bad with her seat and back curved into the wide part of the pithos and her feet and head supported by the smaller bottom and neck. She suspected it would be worse when the jar was straightened but chose to anticipate a leisurely afternoon in Aram's lush courtyard with its soothing fountains. Soon she would be recovering in luxury, rather than in this dusty center of commerce.

After the gates creaked open, she heard animals' hooves and cart wheels approaching her hiding place. She hunkered down as far into the jar as possible and prepared for it to be shifted.

A familiar voice said, "I'll load this one. You get the other two." Slowly Ctesias righted the pithos before lifting it with a grunt and carefully setting it in the back of the cart. "I didn't remember rope to lash them together, so I'll sit back here and make sure they don't fall and break," he told the driver.

Ctesias' hand gripped the rim of her jug as the driver moved his charges into the line of conveyances exiting the caravansary. The jolting found every sore spot on her body, but she clenched her jaw and focused on freedom, relaxing as the animals settled into a slow walk on the street outside the hostelry. The last sound she heard from the caravansary was a bass voice bidding farewell to the departing caravans. *Dael!*

Judith closed her eyes against the fear, like a shooting pain, that she would never be free of her memories.

Chapter 57

Hadassah paused from Passover preparations when a shadow blocked the spring sunshine shining in the open door. "Abba, I've been waiting for our lamb. It will take many hours..." She turned from the bed of coals at her hearth, the remaining words dying on her lips.

"Your father was detained by temple business, so I brought your lamb." Joiada shuffled from one foot to the other outside the door.

Swallowing surprise, Hadassah beckoned him to enter. "Thank you. Father does tend to forget things, and this *will* take hours to roast." She smiled slightly. "If you'd be willing to hold it, I'll slip the spit in." Grabbing the metal rod, she deftly inserted it. She reached to take the meat, but Joiada placed the metal ends on the upright forks in the cook fire.

"It's a bit heavy. A good-sized lamb. Will your sisters' families be joining you for *Pesach?*"

Amazed by his friendliness, Hadassah answered, "No, but some who returned with us, who have no family living here, will share the Pesach feast with us. My sisters will eat with their husband's families. I'll get to see them later this week. We're thankful Miriam can travel."

"Has her ankle healed?"

"Almost. She rode a donkey most of the way. She doesn't have the strength she had."

"We'll petition Adonai for more strength." Joiada bowed as he exited. "Have a joy-filled celebration, Hadassah, and please wish your sisters the same from me and my family."

Hadassah couldn't say a word. She could only stare.

Jarah bustled around the chamber they used whenever Oren served at the temple. With Eliezer contentedly sitting in a corner banging a wooden spoon, Tova set the food on a low table. The guests would recline on sheepskin while they ate the lengthy meal.

"Since you're the youngest, Tova, you can ask the questions. That way you'll know them to teach Eliezer."

"What questions?" Tova inquired.

"There are five. The first one is: Why is this night different from all other nights?"

"I can remember that. I think I even know the answer. It's because we're celebrating our deliverance from slavery in Egypt."

"Exactly," Jarah beamed.

During the feast, as Tova remembered every one of the questions and Oren answered them, Jarah basked in contentment. Although she missed Hannah's piping voice reciting the questions, Jarah was proud of her pupil. Soon Eliezer would ask the questions, and then her child would be old enough to assume that duty.

She touched her belly gently. *Has Adonai blessed us with a son or a daughter?* The child would arrive during the grape harvest, around the time Eliezer celebrated his first year of life.

∞ ∞ ∞

Ezra warmly welcomed Ariel and Gili to his home and accepted two skins of wine from their vineyard. They reclined around a low table topped with spring flowers, two platters of artfully arranged vegetables, and bowls of dipping sauce—one sweet and the other sour. Naama, Adin, and Hadassah brought lamb and cooked eggs as they joined them at the celebratory table.

As they ate the bitter herbs which symbolized slavery, Naama noticed Hadassah appeared happier and more relaxed than she had ever seen her. *She's recovering from her loss. I will too.*

She turned to take the goblet of wine from her husband. His hand brushed hers as he relinquished it. She glanced up into his eyes and rejoiced at the love shining in them. She sipped the results of their labor. Since it was this year's vintage, it wasn't aged, but it was refreshing.

As the company finished the succulent lamb, they talked of the plagues and deliverance. "Moses and our ancestors' departure from Egypt seems more real because of the trek we made last year," Ariel said.

"Now we've experienced God's deliverance firsthand," Gili agreed.

"Me especially," Hadassah added softly. "Not only from the harem, but also here in our land, from that Persian.

"What do you mean?" Gili asked.

"Two moons ago, Hadassah was chased as she returned from a trip to the market. She climbed the wall and balanced on a stone until her pursuers had almost caught her. Then she leaped to safety while the rock fell and crushed one of them," Ezra explained.

"About two months back, Bactrians attacked us in our own vineyard. Turns out the men were looking for our neighbor Benjamin, but they settled for us," Gili said.

"It seems like we would have had more trouble on our long, dangerous trip, but it's been worse since we reached Yehud," Adin observed.

"Who knows what unseen dangers we were delivered from?" mused Hadassah.

"We do have much to be thankful for. Let's end our celebration with a prayer," Ezra said. "O Most High, we praise you tonight for saving us from slavery to the Egyptians long ago, but also from the foreign power of Persia in our lifetimes. 'You have delivered us from the hand of the enemy and ambushes by the way.' You are the God of signs and wonders, who has worked on our behalf with Your strong and outstretched arm. We are Your servants."

"Amen and amen."

Acknowledgments

Thanks to:

Eileen Feldman, for jotting notes about Jericho during her trip to Israel
Lynda DePasecreta, for researching grape vines
Debbie Cossette and Amie Bedgood, for obstetrics expertise
My mother, Sharon Spires, for reading and commenting on several drafts
Fellow author Bruce Judisch, for critiquing my manuscript
New Braunfels Writer's Guild
Irene and the Nashua Christian Writers' Group

If you enjoyed *Such Deliverance as This*, *Such Redemption as This* continues the saga of Hadassah, Jarah, Naama, and Judith. Hadassah and Naama's family stories intertwine with Queen Esther's in the first book of the Such a Hope series *Such a Time as This*.

Naama paused from knotting the blue and tan rug to lift her face and soak up the sun. Fat buds burst from healthy grape vines as far as she could see.

Contentment seeped into her soul, and a smile lighted her face. She had loathed this place. Feared it would not support the family she desired, this scrap of land in *Yehud* that drew her husband Ariel from their home and family in Susa.

Her *em* told her returning to the Promised Land of the Jews would be a blessing. As always, her mother was right. Fourteen years later Naama could finally appreciate her wisdom.

Bees buzzed in springtime flowers. Yael had planted purple spears in a cracked pot and placed it in the courtyard of their limestone cottage. Their home had grown from one rude room to three spaces surrounding an open courtyard. Stout branches spanned the central area. Leafy vines provided shade in the summer, but allowed sunlight to warm the space during cooler months.

Toddler Ebin slept under a wool blanket in a sheltered corner. Naama's oldest daughters Yael and Raisa were fetching water from Gibeon's well. Seven-year-old Saul and five-year-old Nasha were playing in the vineyard but would return soon for dinner.

Neighing alerted Naama to strangers on the path winding through the vineyard. Yael and Raisa appeared first, eyes wide in pale faces. "There's a man here to see you, em," ten-year-old Raisa said.

Naama rose and brushed blue fibers from her robe. Laying one hand on each of her daughters, she greeted a finely dressed Ammonite with a small retinue of servants.

"It's a fine vineyard," he said. "Larger and healthier than the last time I was here."

Fingers of fear snatched at Naama as she struggled to remember him.

"It was before your time," he explained. "Could I have a drink?"

Responding to the note of command in his voice, Yael scurried inside for a cup, scooped water from her clay pot, and offered it to the mounted man. He drank and passed it to the younger man on his right. The two shared a family resemblance, but the teen looked kinder than his haughty father.

"I've come on a business matter."

"My husband's not home presently, sir. We expect him any time."

"I am Tobiah of Rabbah. I was conducting business in Jerusalem and decided to stop here in Gibeon to look after my sister's affairs. This vineyard was the dowry of my sister Judith when she married Benjamin son of Isaak. He divorced her but did not return the land nor its price."

Naama sank to a bench. *Where is Ariel? How would he answer this man?*

"I don't know anything about this. Judith only lived here for a short time when my family first arrived. Benjamin moved away about a year after." The poor man had up and left one winter's day, unable to deal with the memories of his wife and dead daughter.

"My sister owns this property. It's in this marriage contract." The man held up a clay tablet. "She has no desire to turn you out of your home. She'd like payment of fifty *shekels*."

Naama gasped. Ariel kept five silver shekels in the house. He was in Jerusalem selling aged wine and purchasing supplies. He might return with fifteen more. "We...we don't have that much money. Could you camp for the night and speak with my husband and the elders tomorrow?" *Please, Lord, bring Ariel home.*

"I have business to attend. This matter has already consumed the best hours of the day."

"Could I pay part of the price now and the rest later?"

"It needs to be at least half."

Naama staggered into the house and shook their coins out of a carved box. Maybe there would be more than she thought. No, only three. *Ariel must have needed the other two for his trip. How much would he bring home? Surely not twenty-two shekels.* She frantically searched their quarters, looking for anything of value. Her rugs were valuable, but none were complete except an old rug her mother wove years ago. It wouldn't be worth much now.

She returned to find Tobiah eying Yael wolfishly. Swallowing hard, she held out a bag with the three coins. "This is all we have. My husband is selling wine and will bring more."

"How many jugs of wine did he have to sell?"

"Ten jugs of aged wine."

"They won't bring twenty-two shekels," he said harshly.

"No," she admitted, eyes downcast.

"I'll take the girl." He pointed to Yael. "How old are you?"

"Twelve," Yael squeaked.

"A young female servant is worth about fifteen shekels."

"She's betrothed, sir."

"Maybe the bridegroom's family will redeem her."

Naama turned to Raisa and whispered, "Run to David's house. Tell them what's happening. Ask for him and his kinsmen to come *immediately*. If you don't see Gili, ask someone to look for him and send him to the vineyard. Take the little ones with you, except for Ebin. I'll keep him here."

"I'm sure they'll be able to help," Naama announced to her unwanted visitors, trying to keep her voice steady. "I need to make bread. If you'd like to rest in the shade, they'll arrive soon." She picked up her slumbering son and retreated to her indoor hearth with Yael, away from prying eyes.

"Em?" Yael's brown eyes shone with fear. Naama wrapped an arm around her petite firstborn. "Em, are they going to take me away? David doesn't have any money. His father's been sick so long." Her shoulders began to shake as she cried silently.

"I know, child, but I pray he will bring his Uncle Enoch and he'll know what to do."

"They don't have money either..."

"Pray, Yael, and while you pray make some more barley meal." Naama handed her the mortar and pestle. "I'm going to use all you made yesterday."

"Are we making enough for the men outside?"

"Not on your life!"

The unleavened bread was browning on a stone when Raisa reappeared. "David, Enoch, and Samuel are outside with those awful men. I couldn't find Gili."

"Good job, Raisa. Where are the little ones?"

"David's Aunt Mary kept them with her."

"Praise be to Adonai! Raisa, you stay here and make sure the bread doesn't burn. When it's done, put another slab of dough on the stone. Feed Ebin if he gets cranky, but stay in here with your brother, no matter what."

"Yes, Em."

"Come, Yael." Naama took her trembling arm and squeezed it reassuringly. Yael's pleading eyes connected with hers.

As they walked silently into the space in front of the court-yard, they heard Enoch arguing, "You can't swoop into a Jewish village and take a daughter of Judah."

"This debt has been owed my family for thirteen years," Tobiah retorted.

"It was Judith's dowry. Where is she?" Enoch asked.

"I'm collecting it on her behalf."

"Why now, after all these years?" David asked.

"My father recently passed into the next life. I've been sorting through his business affairs and found this tablet."

"May I see it?" Samuel, the only literate one in their group, requested. Tobiah handed it to him. After reading it, Samuel admitted, "This is the marriage contract for Judith the Ammonite. Her dowry was this vineyard. The bride price was goats. It specifies the vineyard is Judith's in the event of divorce."

"My sister was divorced and cast out of this community. She has no desire to remain the owner of this vineyard or deal with tenants. She wants the cost of the vineyard. Fifty shekels is a fair price."

"It is a fair price," Enoch said, "But requiring it with no notice while the head of the family is gone is *not*."

"It's been thirteen years. We could ask for interest."

"I'll go!" The words burst out of Yael. *Maybe, somehow, David and her family could gather fifty shekels. They would never be able to pay thirteen years' interest too.*

Naama froze. "No, please. Wait for my husband to return."

"I have no more time for this matter," Tobiah said harshly. "You've paid me three shekels. These villagers brought five more. I'll take the girl as a slave for now. Redeem her after this year's harvest for fifteen shekels. You'll owe me twenty-seven more." He motioned to his men who mounted quickly.

The young man pulled Yael up behind him on his fine chestnut mare. Stunned, she sat like a sack of grain.

"Yael, hold onto him so you don't fall off," David said.

"Wait, she'll need another robe and a few things." Spinning on her heel, Naama rushed into their sleeping space and grabbed a robe and tunic, stuffing them into a cracked goatskin bag.

When she reached her daughter, she clasped her hand while pressing the bag into it. "Go with God, daughter."

Yael didn't have time to reply as the riders whirled their mounts and trotted up the road.

www.ingramcontent.com/pod-product-compliance
Lightning Source LLC
Chambersburg PA
CBHW022005170626
46808CB00001B/296